Blue Conspiracy

John F Plimmer

Liberty may be endangered by the abuse of liberty, but also by the abuse of power –
James Madison

To Ellie – A true friend

Author's Note

Blue Conspiracy is a story based on a series of true real-life events. A great deal of fiction has been added to provide drama expediency and to portray a tale, which I am sure the reader will find more fascinating than if I had just related to facts alone.

However, the severity of the various activities to which the main character is subjected to in the work, is a true reflection of what actually took place during the occurrences which really happened.

Names and places have been changed to avoid embarrassment, and the principle subject of the story, Jean Goodman never existed.

If any name contained within the work is the same as any living or past person, then such is the result of co-incidence and not intention.

The lady whose role is portrayed in the book by Jean Goodman, is now living a peaceful life in retirement, having gone on to achieve a great many wonderful and inspiring things, following her break from the police service, a job she gave her life to, and for which she still holds fond memories. Has she fully recovered from her ordeal as depicted in the story? No, and she never will.

Chapter One

It was the night everything was supposed to have fallen into place; the night I would finally piece together the complex and highly specialised world of the Police Hostage Negotiator, a small exclusive group whose very existence commanded respect of the highest order. I yearned to research the subject, and those individuals who participated in such peremptory elitism, intending to eventually finalise my findings in book form.

I had ardently left the comfort of my small country cottage to meet one of the country's top detectives, and I might add, the first female ever to successfully complete, probably the most demanding and gruelling policing course at the Hendon Training Centre. Help was on its way, in the shape and form of, Detective Chief Superintendent Jean Goodman. Following months of turning me down flat, the high-profile lady had finally agreed to meet up and share her knowledge and experiences over the past decade or so, with the small tape recorder I had in my pocket.

I became so engrossed with the black shiny puddles of water, slowly being transformed into miniature lakes around my rain sodden trainers, I hadn't noticed the woman I had known for most of my professional life, was well overdue for our meeting. A quick glance at the Mickey Mouse wristwatch my mother had bought me one Christmas, almost half a century before, told me that Miss Goodman was late. The antique on my wrist, which had been repaired more times than I could remember, in fact confirmed she was some twenty minutes late. So, where the bloody hell was she? If all the coppers in the country were as unpunctual as their top detective, it was no wonder they always seemed to fail to attend, until it was all over.

There I was, standing alone, trying hard to shelter beneath an overhang outside the newly built International Railway Station. I couldn't take advantage of the drier climate inside from fear that I might miss my very important date. At least I was silhouetted against the bright lights illuminating the pedestrian elevators and spacious landings inside the main entrance to the building. Not that the old railway station had really been in need of a dozen or so bulldozers to callously bring it down to ground level, before the modern structure appeared like the Phoenix rising out of the ashes. Heaven forbid; the original complex had only been servicing the public on behalf of British Rail, for less than the previous twelve years or so. But people had to make money, including a few dubious local councillors, whose personal bank balances wouldn't have suffered much from such a large rebuilding scheme, hence the reason for yet another new railway station, or so I assumed.

The minutes ticked by. The rain continued unabated. Miss Goodman was half an hour late, give or take a few minutes either side of the long hands across Mickey's face. Perhaps she'd changed her mind and just hadn't bothered to ring? Most coppers were like that. You know the kind of individuals. Good at throwing a dozen balls in the air at the same time and not deciding which one to catch until they'd almost hit the ground. They used to call it 'crisis management' when I was a young Detective Superintendent. Having said that, I was perhaps the closest friend she had in those earlier and balmy days, or so I hoped at that particular moment, and she was well aware of the energy I'd previously put into researching the subject I was eager to begin writing up.

I drew some comfort from the thought that any lengthy wait would be well rewarded at the end. There was no one better suited to discuss the subject with, than the lady herself. Hostage Negotiators shared a kind of secret world within the police service and was just the kind of topic I believed would finally launch my writing career straight into the charts. So, I certainly wasn't over bothered about having to toy with the elements for a few extra minutes, although I must admit to regretting not having worn something more substantial than a black woollen pullover and pair of denim trousers.

The rain continued with a vengeance and when the same corporation bus inspector decided to retrace his earlier steps, walking straight past me, casting a sceptical eye towards where I stood, I began to feel uncomfortable. I mean to say, why shouldn't someone stand in the pouring rain, and remain there after at least three buses had stopped outside the double fronted door just a few yards to my right, and then drive off leaving me frozen to the spot? Perhaps the official thought I was planning on commandeering one his buses? Anyway, my patience finally began to wear thin and another ten minutes passed by, without any sign of my elusive female top cop.

I gazed down at those ever-increasing black puddles again, seeking inspiration but finding none. It was time to move on and just mark up yet another failure along life's long and dreary road. My upper regions were dry enough, thanks to the railway station's overhang, but my trouser legs were beginning to resemble a couple of sponges. And I hadn't felt my toes since God knows when. As I attempted to restore some life into a network of stiffened joints, I only hoped that, Jean Goodman hadn't been hit by a train or suddenly carried off by a large swooping eagle. The interior warmth made me feel slightly more human, stepping through the automatic glass panelled door, into the bright lights of the large and spacious ground floor hallway, with its pedestrian elevators and car park ticket machines.

"Is that you, Ray?"

"Hello, John."

"Is she about? I arranged to meet her at the International railway station about an hour ago, but she hasn't turned up."

"She's tied up with the Special Projects Team, I can't say too much over the phone," explained Jean's evanescent brother.

Well, cobblers to you mate, I thought, returning the mobile phone to my tight-fitting trouser pocket. Why was it, everything these coppers ever did was a state secret. And what the bloody hell was the Special Projects Team? It sounded like a convention for designer draughtsmen. Still, at least she could have phoned to let me know rather than leave me standing there, mimicking a recently sacked umbrella salesman. There was only one thing for it, a one-way ticket home on the next train outward bound.

Thanks to my daughter's meddling, every time someone rang my mobile, a farmyard cockerel began to crow, which was somewhat embarrassing when I just happened to be standing in the middle of a crowd, all waiting to catch the same train. But there it was again, and I frantically retrieved the twenty first century's most marketable product from that incommodious tight-fitting pocket. By the time I'd flipped the portable phone open, it was sounding off like a screaming bird protecting her young. It was amazing how nobody seemed to hear and just surrounded me, all looking into empty space, or down at various wrist watches. I could have been committing a murder right there in front of my fellow travellers' eyes, and still they would have remained staring at nothing in particular; or checking the time.

"Yes!" I almost shouted down the mouthpiece of the small contraption.

"It's Raymond again, John."

"I would never have guessed."

"Sorry, I couldn't say much before in case they had the phones tapped."

Now I was all ears. The crowd around me was instantly forgotten and the lad suddenly held my undivided attention.

"They came early this morning and arrested Jean. She's been taken to Police Headquarters and I've no idea when she'll be back."

Was the lad kidding or what? Was this some kind of April Fool's joke, only it was October. I quickly looked around me, half expecting to see a cluster of former colleagues, sniggering and pointing fingers towards the prat who'd been set up, namely me.

Detective Chief Superintendent Jean Goodman, the most innovative and hardest working number one dick the police service had ever known, arrested? That kind of news would certainly put my project on Hostage Negotiators in the shade. It just had to be a huge prank? Problem was, Raymond Goodman wasn't the kind of bloke who messed around. I'd known Jean's brother almost as long as I'd been acquainted with his sister, and an Egyptian mummy would have had a greater sense of humour that good old, Ray.

"You still there, John?"

"Yes, just a little bewildered by what you've just told me."

"Shall I get her to call you when she gets home."

"Er, yes, I suppose so." I had to think, which at that precise moment was a nigh on impossibility. Be fair, I'd just been informed of what could be the greatest scandal ever recorded in the annals of cops and robbers.

"Tell her I'll keep my mobile on." What else could I say? In all probability she wouldn't give a toss whether I was contactable or not, but at that very precise moment, my inquisitive senses were on full alert.

Having wandered aimlessly from one platform to another, in total shock, and having obviously missed my homeward bound train, I decided to catch one travelling in the opposite direction. Within a short space of time, I found myself drying out in the public lounge of a small hotel owned by some friends of mine.

Graham Cardigan had experienced a few problems of his own during his lifetime. Having weighed in at something like thirty-six stone, one operation to reduce his stomach to the size of an egg had meant he'd starved himself over a twelve-month period, losing something in the region of twenty-five stone. Now, you might well think, the lad should have been given the 'Weight Watchers' gong for the year, having accomplished such a feat, and currently looking like a turkey just back from a one-hundred-mile race. But the only result, Graham had accomplished, was to spend most of the remainder of his life, frequently running in and out of various hospitals, like a guinea pig for all to examine. In fact, I doubt if there is anyone alive on this planet, who'd been subjected to as much pain and suffering as the slimmed down version of my mate, Graham.

Obviously, I couldn't tell him anything about Chief Superintendent Jean Goodman's dilemma because I had no idea myself. I couldn't even remember what we talked about, knocking back a couple of pints of lager with my thoughts constantly focused on what the hell was going on inside the local police force. Then that bloody cockerel sounded off again and a short verbal message from the lady herself, invited me to her house.

A brief train ride and a couple of taxies were soon put to good use, and by the time I finally met up with the same senior detective I was supposed to have met a few hours earlier, midnight was rapidly approaching.

Her brother, Raymond, opened the front door and led the way into a rectangular shaped lounge. He had always been an emaciated looking bloke, with more hair on his chin than his head, but whose loyalty to his sister was virtually combative. There was the usual three-tiered settee positioned under the window. The usual few paintings decorating the walls, with an ornamental brick-built fireplace, and mandatory French windows at the far end of the room. What made the lounge different from most others was the figure of a broken woman, standing very unsteadily in the centre of the room, facing me. She was wearing a matching dark blue jacket and skirt with a white satin blouse pinned at the top by a Duke of Edinburgh's Gold Award brooch, a memento of her younger days trekking through the Welsh hills.

Jean still had her shoulder length chestnut hair tied up at the back, which was her usual appearance when engaged in official duties, but she was a lot different from when I had last seen her. The look of despair etched across her corrugated face was obvious, and her dark brown saucer like eyes just stared as if looking into some invisible void. She resembled a person who had just realised she'd copped a bullet between the shoulder blades, from which she would never recover.

"What the hell..." I gasped.

"It's terrible," she interrupted, obviously in desperation, "I don't know what's happened. I've been arrested and they've kept me for most of the day at Headquarters, asking questions about Arthur Grainger." Her voice was solemn, almost a whisper, and most certainly overflowing with chagrin.

"Who's Arthur Grainger?" I asked, instantly remembering some old guy she'd mentioned before to me. Hadn't he been pestering her, writing a book or something about her life in the police? Hadn't an, Arthur Grainger telephoned me at home a couple of years before, asking me to provide some kind of personal reference? Of course, he'd been trying to get some Honorary Award on, Jean's behalf, conning me into believing he'd obtained the Chief Constable's approval. No serving cop could be given any kind of external Award without the authority of the top jolly, and when I'd discovered Jean's admirer hadn't actually had his application authorised, I'd phoned him back and introduced the man to a string of metaphors he probably wouldn't have been acquainted with.

"That old man I've mentioned to you before, who kept ringing my phone and dropping off gifts outside the front door," she continued in a shaky voice, obviously no longer concerned about the state of her pinned up hair, which resembled a thatch of recently reaped straw, covered in some obnoxious deposit normally found in fields containing cattle.

"So?"

"He's made a complaint that I've taken those gifts off him because we had a mutual relationship."

"And?"

"That's it, that's the truth. I don't know anything else."

I asked her to sit down and start at the beginning, but she was reluctant to do so, sit down I mean, obviously too distressed to do anything except just stand there.

The story then unfolded, as she told me about the most bizarre series of events I had ever been witness to. A series of events which had begun at 6.30 a.m. that morning and had been responsible for turning the past eighteen hours or so, into the blackest day of her life.

Chapter Two

From the lady's general demeanour, it was painfully obvious she was overawed by distress. She needed to talk to someone about the hideous and macabre series of events, which had obviously created a psychological imbalance in her highly intelligent mind, if only temporary. I sat and listened intently as her story unfolded, in between spasmodic outbursts of tears and physical shaking.

It had been six thirty that morning, when she'd first heard her front door bell sound off. As she glided across the small landing, finding it difficult to run both arms through the sleeves of her dressing gown, her mind was still concentrating on the paperwork she thought she'd left strewn across the downstairs lounge floor, having left it there just a couple of hours before. It wasn't important; whoever was banging on her door so early on this particular Saturday morning evidently was. The top detective was certain of one thing; coppers rattling their truncheons on her threshold so early in the morning, meant only one thing, the rest of her weekend might just as well be cancelled there and then.

'Must be another murder,' she thought, as she reached the bottom stair and looked at the two human figures silhouetted on the other side of the glass-panelled door. That was the only logical reason for such an unsolicited early morning call.

She forced a smile and stepped across the hallway carpet, trying hard to disguise her annoyance at having been awakened from her slumber, so prematurely and on a rare day of rest. Jean left the safety chain in place, as she slowly unlocked the door, trying hard to shake off the drowsiness that would have been apparent to those she was about to confront.

With some surprise, the force's Head of CID was greeted by the normally supercilious, Superintendent Robert Snipe and his deputy, Chief Inspector, Len Tallis. They were in charge of the Deputy Chief Constable's Special Projects Team, so what the hell would they be doing chasing up a murder? The only game they were interested in was investigating other cops.

She closed the door and released the chain before reopening it and asking what kind of job required her attention at such an unsociable hour.

Bob Snipe was a small man who presented a serious, almost stony look across a pale complexion. Both men were wearing the usual business-like attire, suits with ties to match, and facial features that would have been more befitting a pair of undertakers. They stood a little rigid as the Superintendent explained in his high-pitched voice to his senior female officer, that there wasn't a job that needed her attention. In fact, he and his team of internal investigators had come for her.

"We've had a formal complaint that you have deceived an, Arthur Grainger, and he's given you gifts, items of jewellery which you have obtained by deception, when you falsely said you had a mutually exclusive relationship with him."

Well now, that was quite an opening salvo. Imagine being greeted by such a verbal onslaught at your front door at gone six in the morning. At first, and quite understandable, Jean wondered whether he'd left his fancy dress at home. The man certainly appeared nervous and slightly breathless, obviously not having spent too much time rehearsing his initial address. In fact, the meaning of his words hadn't quite penetrated through into the senior detective's mind, and she just stood there in silence, having some difficulty in maintaining her smile. The only question she was thinking of at that time was, 'What the bloody hell are you on about my lad?'

A search warrant was produced, telling the lady of the house that 'someone' had complained about her ripping off an elderly pensioner, and giving half the bloody police force the right to go through her house in search of gifts she had supposedly received from an admirer.

"Unbelievable," I said to no one in particular, as she continued her story.

Grasping both hands tightly together, in an effort to stop them from trembling, she then told me that, without hesitation, she'd handed over some items of jewellery, which had previously been left outside her front door, by the man himself, 'Storming Arthur,' a name she preferred to call the elderly pensioner because of his persistent character.

Her brother, Raymond confirmed he'd actually returned the same gifts to his sister's elderly stalker. Unfortunately, the generous donator had never been able to take 'no' for an answer, and had in fact, returned them by leaving small parcels outside the front of Jean's house.

"Why should I want more jewellery?" she said to me, "I have my own and my mother's upstairs. I hardly wear the stuff."

That seemed to be a reasonable assumption to me, but I was still waiting for the coup de grace, the real reason why she'd just probably had her whole career destroyed.

She continued her briefing, as if I was some sort of High Court official, sitting in judgement on the events to which she had been unscrupulously and immorally subjected. For my part, I was slightly mesmerised, if not puzzled by the whole affair.

"I've been making arrangements with Father John, to have the gifts returned to the family through the church."

"Who's Father John?" I asked, ignorant of the fact that he was her local priest, which she quickly confirmed.

Anyway, following the knock on her door by the boys in blue, only then did her nightmare really take off.

"I'd been working on some confidential papers until four in the morning and they were scattered about the floor, here in the lounge," she said. "I asked Bob Snipe, if I could secure them before he let the rest of his officers inside the house, but he told me to leave them."

"And did you?" I asked.

The besmirched woman shook her head. "No, I put them away,

before going back upstairs to get dressed."

Sensible girl I thought, trying to think how I would have reacted in the same circumstances, coming to the conclusion that I would probably have finished up being carted off to a prison cell, having committed various unlawful acts of physical violence, on those who were invading my privacy on the basis of such a flimsy excuse.

Although the tears failed to dry up, as she paced her way through her experiences, the real stab to the heart became obvious when she once again acknowledged that the intruders were officers from her own force; the majority being constables. Individuals, whom she had known for some years, worked with and even shared a few jokes with, from time to time. As if that wasn't enough to throw her into a dizzy spin, some of her unwelcome visitors had previously submitted grievances against, Jean and other senior officers. Every police force had them; professional moaners who never did any wrong, in their own eyes that is.

Chief Superintendent Malcolm Richards arrived at the house. He was a Superintendent Association's representative who had been summoned there to act on, Jean Goodman's behalf, for the purpose of supporting the lady in a welfare capacity. He had also known, Jean for a number of years and was perhaps the most trusted bloke she could have at her side, at such a critical time, having vast experience in supporting other police officers who had found themselves trapped within inescapable nets of major traumatic incidents. He was undoubtedly a proven and credible soldier, when representing officers' welfare interests.

Jean then explained how she had stood with her brother in an upstairs bedroom, watching a couple of male officers concentrate on the contents of her bedside table drawers. They missed nothing, sifting through personal items, including knickers, bras and sanitary wear. At one point they even took an old x-ray of their suspect, and held it up to a window, both gawping at the skeletal details, and enjoying the odd sarcastic and hurtful comment.

Raymond Goodman sat in silence, nodding his head at his sister's vociferous objections, but to no avail. There was worse to come.

I was aware that, Jean, had recently lost her mother, a lady who had suffered greatly, before death had released her from a prolonged illness. Edna Goodman had lived with her daughter throughout her painful ordeal. Although the amount of time the Detective Chief Superintendent had spent at home had been extremely limited, the Head of CID, having worked about eighteen hours in every twenty-four, had devoted what freedom she had, nursing her mother. Those weirdos who were now ploughing through her private life, like vultures seeking out a nest full of harmless sparrows, must have really been turned on when they came across a bundle of medical accessories and supplies, which had been used to support her mother's incontinence.

Of course, the kind of sick jokes and twisted puns quickly followed, leaving the senior female detective embarrassed and grieving. So much so, she had to sit at the top of the stairs, alongside her brother, trying hard to close her ears to the jibes that were drifting across the landing, from inside the room in which she slept.

"Unbelievable." As the story unfolded, I began to feel personally ashamed I had once belonged to the same organisation.

Private financial documents were scrupulously examined, including wage packets. Comments were made about the salary received by a Detective Chief Superintendent, in particular the one whose house they were defiling, under the legal guise of a search warrant.

At one stage, Raymond Goodman found he couldn't take any more. Pacing across the landing, towards the bedroom being searched, he stood defiantly in the doorway, keeping both arms down at his sides, but fists clenched tightly, in readiness to lash out at the aggravators who were still sporting contumelious smiles and muttering antagonising quips. His eyes pierced through the hostile atmosphere, landing on one officer in particular, who was thumbing through a pile of receipts, recovered from a drawer beneath the divan bed.

"God, she's got receipts going back to 1997 here," the man sarcastically quipped.

"Here's another from Ideal World, and another from Ideal World. Is that all she does, shop at Ideal World?"

My own response to such unprofessional arrogance, would have been far more aggressive than, Raymond Goodman's. Jean's brother felt a burning desire to walk in and thrust the paperwork straight up the bloke's arse, but thankfully, knowing that was exactly the kind of action these deluded reprobates would have been hoping for, managed to restrain himself.

"That's all she can do, she works very long hours. Something you people would know little about," he gasped from the doorway.

Of course, they showered him with their self-important glances. Most conceited cops were good at that. Then came the sort of crooked smiles that always invited someone to come in closer, and take a dig whenever they felt like it, the consequences being extremely detrimental to the individual being chided. But, having spent the past twenty plus years rubbing shoulders with this kind of low life, the last thing he was going to do was hand them a ticket, which would have justified their presence in his sister's house.

"Unbelievable."

A female Inspector appeared from somewhere and noticed one of her male officers reading through a bundle of personal bank statements belonging to the lady of the house.

"We are not looking at banking," the woman said, "I've told you before now, we are not looking at banking."

She might just as well have been speaking from the German Bunker on the Island of Jersey. The officer was either deaf or in complete ignorance of her presence inside the bedroom, and just continued with his study of the financial documents. And why not, who gives a toss about what's contained in a search warrant, particularly one that restricts the search to 'items of jewellery'. More importantly, who gives a toss about what some woman Inspector's opinions are? Such an adverse way of thinking was embedded within their culture.

"Unbelievable."

According to Jean, other documents examined by the cops during that traumatic period, included divorce papers, wills and other papers relevant to her mother's death, including consultant's reports concerning an internal medical examination the orator had undergone on a previous occasion. It was as if her whole personal life was being breached in such a way it was akin to being raped, and by her own officers, which I found to be astounding.

Her brother then interrupted the narration by presenting us both with a glass of brandy. Jean didn't touch hers, so I drank both glasses, without even thinking about anything beyond the bizarre story, which was sounding more like some war time script, in which the German SS invaded some collaborators hiding place.

"Throughout the whole ordeal, I felt like a victim of some cruel and criminal act," she explained nervously, "I felt a mixture of shock, anger and total bewilderment, not really appreciative of what was taking place, and not believing the reasons why they were there, inside my house, defiling my very existence."

That was quite a statement, but in my view, she was still experiencing those same feelings. Her hands had never stopped shaking, her voice had never stopped quivering, and the lady certainly couldn't have tried any harder, although unsuccessfully, to stop bitterly weeping. In fact, she reminded me of someone who was grieving the loss of a loved one and had no idea how to deal with it.

Towards the end of that part of her ordeal, she and her brother were escorted back down the stairs into the lounge, where, Snipe and Tallis had remained throughout, with Jean's representative, Malcolm Richards.

Robert Snipe told his boss that she would have to go with him, adding, "If you don't come with us voluntary, we will have to arrest you." In fact, I commented that his words actually constituted an arrest.

The Detective Chief Superintendent continued with her story, telling me that she had stiffened and given an immediate response. "Arrest me, what on earth are you on about?"

The lady's antagoniser then suggested, "There are sufficient grounds to arrest you.   You will have to come with us to be further questioned at a local police station."

Acting in accordance with the high rank she held, she immediately suggested that such a move wouldn't be discreet or professional, and asked if she could be taken to another force area. Jean was fully aware that where ever they took her, she would be scrutinised like some poor creature on display in some travelling circus.

Snipe then turned to the others present and explained, "If we go to another force area we haven't got the power to detain her."

That part of the unfolding story confused me somewhat. After all, we weren't talking about a known Drugs Baron here; or some serial killer or armed robber. The Superintendent in charge of the search party had just arrested a woman who was his Head of CID, and who had completed more than thirty years of outstanding police service. As a young probationer, many years before, Jean Goodman had been the force's pin-up girl. Her face had been plastered all over town on various recruitment posters, and her organisation had wallowed in the positive publicity she'd achieved as a result of meetings with Royalty, and just about every other celebrity who'd been knocking about at that time.

Chief Superintendent Malcolm Richards must have experienced the same feelings when he asked why, Snipe and his band of party goers, couldn't leave the interview until the following Monday. "I mean," he conceded, "She's given you all the items; she's been honest and it's not urgent to interview her."

Snipe replied guardedly, "It needs to be dealt with today, the DCC wants it dealt with today," referring to the Deputy Chief Constable, Adrian Plum. Now there was a man who, according to his history of Employment Tribunals, had never believed in taking any prisoners alive. According to Jean, that was the first time she'd had any idea that Mr. Plum had been behind the horror show taking place in her home.

Eventually, a decision was reached, whereby the now prisoner, was to be taken to Police Headquarters where the self-congratulating gathering, would continue to interrogate her.

I was still having some difficulty in accepting that the reason for the methods adopted by, what could only be described as an over-reactive group of delinquents, was as a result of allegations concerning the acceptance of gifts from a pensioner. It all seemed, at that time, to be part of a script from a television drama, for which the production team had been badly advised.

I became more confused when, Jean told me that, Robert Snipe had made it quite clear, if she refused to stay at Police Headquarters, she would be arrested and taken to a local police station, before being put on display. You see, the man had already arrested the lady previously, and by making such a further statement, had yet again, arrested her a second time. Where had they got these people from? I had seen higher levels of professionalism in our budgie at home, when attempting to reach a ball of Millett seed hanging from the top of its cage. Still the bizarre game had to be played out, and everybody in that room apparently nodded their heads in full agreement of what the Top Gun was saying.

"Unbelievable."

Amazingly, having downed a couple of brandies and having focused my mind on every word the distraught lady had spoken, I didn't feel the least tired. It was well past one in the morning and a full squadron of SAS combatants couldn't have removed me from that couch at that particular time. I fidgeted a little, but my full receptive faculties patiently waited for the next phase of this incredible and disastrous story to be shared. And, believe me I wasn't disappointed when it came down to basic drama.

Again, according to Jean, she was driven to Police Headquarters by, Malcolm Richards, although she was later to discover that the search team actually remained at her house for an additional two hours, after she had left. Heaven knows why, having already spent six hours plus, going through the place. After all, I can confirm that the woman didn't live in a mansion. This wasn't Balmoral or Blenheim Palace we're discussing. It was one of your usual four-bedroomed detached houses, in they had spent nigh on eight hours going over. I suppose the cops could have argued that they'd had some problems searching under the wallpaper, but who would have believed them? In total, eleven police officers had attended at the house that morning. If that hadn't been enough, there was a gathered assembly, waiting to welcome her at Police Headquarters. It reminded me of the crowds that used to greet the Beatles at the airport, having returned home from a successful tour of the States during the sixties.

"I still can't believe the number of officers that came to my house," she said.

Me and you both, kid.

Chapter Three

Mental and physical exhaustion finally brought that first late night meeting with, Jean Goodman, to an abrupt end, and in response to the lady's invitation, I agreed to return the following morning. This might seem strange to most, but I actually found it difficult to wish her, 'goodnight'. How could you genuinely suggest that a person should have a few peaceful hours of slumber, after just having their lives wrecked? I had no doubt that the following few hours was probably going to be the worst period of her life and following the spectacular intrusion which had taken place earlier that day, the lady's safe domestic domain, would never feel the same again.

I left her standing just inside her front doorway, silhouetted against the light in the hallway and trying hard to force a smile. She was a pathetic figure, very much alone and vulnerable. A once high-profile public figure who had now been cruelly reduced to an archetypal fractious human sample of smouldering ashes. After pacing just a few yards down her driveway, I suddenly felt inadequate, so turned back to face her. Grasping both of her, still trembling hands in mine, I attempted a few soothing words.

"Try not to worry too much, Jean, I find it difficult to imagine how you are feeling right now, but take my word, you will have your day. That, I promise you."

She just faintly nodded, and I left, still feeling inadequate.

As I paced along dark shiny pavements, I couldn't help but think I had just witnessed the fall from grace of a female icon; an institution within the organisation she had devoted her life to. And yet, I had no idea why. From what I had been told, the very people who had once been under her command, had filled her home with a ceaseless commotion of amateurish insolence and cruelty, all in the name of what they would call, 'duty'.

As I continued with my long trek home, I concentrated on parts of the story she'd earlier fumbled her way through, struggling to avoid a minefield of puddles, as a misty rain began to add to the misery of the night's events.

Everything that had taken place, appeared to have happened beneath a dark cloak of enigmatic uncertainty. The mental analysis I was studiously attempting to clarify, seemed to be beyond my reach. What I was convinced of, was that, if the detailed account given to me by, Jean Goodman was accurate, and I had no reason to doubt her synopsis at that time, then there had to be a hidden agenda concealed somewhere beneath the attitude and behaviour of those who had so harshly brought the lady to her knees. Whatever the result of such debased contamination awaited her in the near future, I sensed a pervading condemnation of her character being exhibited throughout the public arena. That could not be avoided after what they had done to her. And that in itself, I knew, would be far more hurtful to the lady than going to prison. For that reason, I found myself in a precarious position. Here I was, with both hands on the tiller of an exclusive horror story, which would undoubtedly cause volcanic eruptions throughout the newspapers readership. And yet, having been told it in confidence, how the bloody hell could I ever write it up?

My pedestrian homeward journey wasn't helped much either, by a chilling night breeze, doing its utmost to compete with the lingering mists. Still I persevered with my analytical reasoning. How could they, her own colleagues, have subjected such a high-ranking officer to the kind of traumatic and disgraceful behaviour she'd been made to suffer? If it came to that, how could any human being act so callously towards another? After all, this was Tony Blair's Britain, not some country labouring under some dictatorial regime, or had I got that one wrong as well.

Another puddle. Another jet of cold water shot up my leg, as I failed to concentrate on where I was placing my size tens. Now I was really starting to get pissed off by this damned weather.

The region she'd served with so much enthusiasm since those early adventurous years during the 1970's, recorded an annual average of almost half a million crimes committed amongst a population of two and a half million people. And, Jean Goodman had been the girl responsible for confronting that lot, almost single handed, during the previous four years in which she had held her current rank and position. Her success could never be surpassed. Perhaps that was the problem? The lady's professional record was well out of the reach of others and would be for a long time to come. Could it be, for that reason only, they had decided to bring her down by using other, more sinister means. You couldn't make this lot up if you tried.

Born in the back streets of an inner-city slum and being one of four kids born to her mother and father, she'd got to know all about life's struggles during her childhood. I recalled the occasions when she had laughed over small childhood experiences. Such as when she had sat at the dinner table with her three siblings, all perched on the edge of their seat, like new-born chicks with their beaks wide open, begging for nourishment, as her mother dished out a watered-down version of soup. And how any new clothes they were given to wear on special occasions, were all hand me downs, including shoes and plimsoles.

That kind of difficult and arduous childhood history, had prepared her well, to later deal with the problems she had been obliged to confront in a sexist, male dominated organisation. Yet, she had succeeded, facing her misguided, and on occasions, jealous critics like a Trojan, without complaint or misgivings. I was aware only too well of her resilience, having worked side by side with her. Two highly spirited young detectives, committed to capturing villains and law breakers, and not giving a tinker's damn about the rest of them.

Those were the days and my mind flew back to various encounters we'd shared as youngsters, trying to come to terms with the criminal mind. Such as the time I found myself trying to arrest a wanted rapist who weighed about 280 pounds. I'd quickly finished up lying on my back in the downstairs front room of some Edwardian terraced house, with Mr. Gigantic doing his utmost to break my scrawny neck. I remembered the adrenaline rush which helped me to turn the Colossus over and reverse our positions, with me on top of him, only to be felled by a violent strike to the back of my head, causing blood to rush out like an active geyser. Jean had missed her target with a large crock vase, managing to hit me instead.

Other than a few skirmishes such as that one, our working relationship had been fairly successful, in fact almost legendary, apart from the occasional demoniac confrontation. Ours had been a love, hate relationship, which sometimes resulted in a particular young lady's hair being matted with chicken and chips or anything else similar I could get my hands on, when in a raging temper. Still, somehow, we had managed to hold it together and had eventually become lifelong trusted pals, and confidantes.

I also recollected on that long walk home, the lady's joy at having completed the arduous task of qualifying as the first female Hostage Negotiator in the country, not knowing what other magnificent feats she was to perform later in her service. Although she had readily told me of the excitement she'd shared with others on the course, she'd explained how SAS combatants had confronted her with more verbal abuse and physical threats than she could ever have imagined were possible, during various training operations. But she'd managed to overcome such testing incidents and successfully passed the Hostage Negotiators course with flying colours.

Had there been any men in her life? Of course, there must have been dozens. After all, she was a woman with feelings, but never foolish enough to allow any relationship to stand in the way of her destiny as a top detective, one whose fame had almost become allegorical, before it had all ended so abruptly.

Perhaps what had happened had been sparked by some kind of misinterpretation of the facts? Of course, I wasn't in any position at that time to pre-judge the situation she was in, but I knew, Jean Goodman well enough, and I also knew that no matter what others might have said, she would never have exposed her career to the kind of foolishness that had been suggested.

Her list of achievements was almost endless. She'd learned her job the hard way, remaining at each level of the promotion ladder long enough to learn and understand, a rarity in a world where recruits felt an urge to reach the top within months rather than years.

In 1999, she had been promoted to Detective Chief Superintendent, making her the first operational female Head of CID in the country. Her role had given her the responsibility of overseeing all major crime incidents, with six Detective Superintendents, sixteen Detective Chief Inspectors and twenty-four Detective Inspectors working to her. The lady's professional domain spanned across forty-three separate interactive units, supported by a total of eight hundred police and civilian support staff. There was also a small matter of having to control a £25 million budget for major crime and informant handling, in addition to a further £2.6 million targeted towards scientific and DNA crime scene submissions. Such highly regarded responsibilities made me shudder, acknowledging the kind of professional commitments which would have gone beyond my own limitations.

Within six months of being appointed as the top detective, she'd successfully assessed both the force and national crime picture, including the political influences and government priorities. Miss Goodman had also completely restructured the Criminal Investigation Department into a more effective law enforcement agency, with stronger communication links and harder working personnel. Her streamlining process was identified by the Home Office and Surveillance Commissioners, as being the kind of centre of excellence they'd been looking for, and which the rest of the country could follow. But it didn't end there.

Jean led the police service on areas which included, sensitive policing techniques, disclosure methods, sex offender and child internet response, family liaison methods and policy, and many others. She'd also been responsible for the in-force training of eight thousand police officers in all criminal-related matters, and revamped regional training programmes connected to Major Incident Rooms, murder investigations, kidnappings, child abuse, sexual crimes, and numerous other sensitive areas of policing. The list of achievements went on, and I knew about them, because I had written pages filled with their individual details.

I had previously been made aware of my former colleague's personal involvement in a recent car bomb attack committed by the 'Real IRA' and which had resulted in a string of convictions. The same lady had urgently put together Islamic Terrorist Major Incident Rooms, following the 11th of September atrocities in New York.

Her personal record over the previous four years read like a Hollywood film script. A serial killer was quickly hunted down, at a time when her desk was filled with reports of other allegations of major crime and police corruption. Jean's personal fame had resulted, not from successful appearances in front of cameras or inquisitive journalists, in fact she'd always shied away from the media, but from the successes she achieved in such a short period of time, on both a local and national level.

Now then, if that lot wasn't enough to justify a salary ten times the size of, Jean Goodman's, there were other phases of her life to be considered. For instance, in addition to her normal eighteen-hour day, she was an active school governor at a local Junior School, where she played a leading role in the compilation of school policies relevant to training, child abuse, special needs, school business planning, performance indicators and measurement strategy. And if there was ever any doubt regarding the lady's working commitment, she was also a voluntary Sunday school teacher, specialising with children between 3 and 14 years of age. If there had ever been a few spare minutes in this woman's hectic life, then she had always had the option of performing her duties as a member of her local Parish Church Council and District Church Committees. Quite a daily routine for a person who was supposed to have gone around ripping old men off, wouldn't you think?

She had once told me that her achievements were based on an ambition to create a transparent environment, which would be responsible for propelling criminal investigation forward towards a more effective future. To create a wider understanding of a need for the co-operation and understanding of staff, the community and outside agency partners. I remember thinking at the time, how impressive and academic it all sounded, not believing for a micro second that she would ever achieve a fraction of her aims, and certainly not within such a male dominated structure. But she did and she had.

It also became known to me later that, Jean Goodman's Criminal Investigation Department was widely regarded as one of 'Flagship' stature, and frequently welcomed senior officers from other forces who wanted to view the working of her Department first hand. Some accolade you might well think. But would she ever be able to return to that powerful position? Would the public once again benefit from the lady's undying commitment towards them? After what had just happened, never in a reign of pigs' pudding.

Already, there were a thousand questions I wanted to ask, urgently. But as the rain increased, I quickened my pace and wished to goodness I'd accepted, Raymond Goodman's offer of a lift home. Not long now, just another fifteen minutes or so of ducking from beneath the branches of one tree to the next, and I would be safely home. If I could manage to switch off the multitude of thoughts racing through my head, I might even be able to snatch a few hours' sleep, which I was convinced was more than, Jean Goodman would be in receipt of, during the remainder of that particular dark and very wet night.

Chapter Four

When I returned to Jean's home the following morning, the dispiriting atmosphere hit me as soon as I walked through the door, which was not surprising, considering the events of the day before. Dark patches around her eyes told their own story, and I was invited to sit at a kitchen table with a mug of coffee placed before me. Jean sat opposite and continued where she'd left off the night before. At least the tears had dried up, although her voice remained nervous and quiet.

As the tale of woe continued to unfold, it quickly became apparent that, Jean Goodman, had been treated by her own people without any consideration having been given to the lady's legal or human rights. I remained appalled at the behaviour of those working under the pretence of being professional investigators.

There was no need to prompt her. I wasn't there, seeking material for a book or newspaper feature. I was there purely as a friend and one who she had shared a great deal of her professional life with. A trusting servant if you like, but one in whom she could confide. And there was no doubt at that time, she certainly needed someone to lean on. Jean bravely outlined exactly, everything she could remember had taken place after leaving her house in, Malcolm Richards car.

When she eventually arrived at Police Headquarters, they found the floor on which the Special Projects team worked had been taped off, in similar fashion to a murder scene, and there were cops posted in the corridor containing the interview room in which the most senior detective was to be interrogated.

She remembered a glib remark made by, Malcolm Richards, confirming he had never before seen so many officers working in that department on a Saturday afternoon. One thing was certain, once inside that building, she was going nowhere, not in the immediate future anyway. And even if she had been tempted to dive for freedom, she would have had to have leapt out of a fifth storey window.

Following a short delay, more professional support came Jean's way in the form of, John Mitchell, a young solicitor sent by the Superintendent's Association to represent the lady's legal interests. The lawyer's initial response to the circumstances surrounding his high-profile client's arrest, was one of total scepticism, and he immediately made his feelings known. The lawyer believed the actions thus far taken against, Jean Goodman, were totally disproportionate to the allegations made against her.

Very quickly, all three, Jean, her solicitor and Malcolm Richards, were ushered into an interview room where audio tapes were waiting to record every word spoken. Superintendent Snipe was assisted by a sergeant and police constable, the latter having already displayed his bizarre sense of humour back at Jean's house, in an upstairs bedroom.

Remember, "God, she's got receipts going back to 1997 here," and "Here's another from Ideal World, and another from Ideal World. Is that all she does, shop at Ideal World?" Well, his Head of CID was hoping the same garrulous joker would make similar irresponsible quips in the presence of her solicitor and welfare representative. Alas, that was not to be, but the team of interrogators were not about to fall short of providing their captive with more controversial and embarrassing behaviour, in their effort to denigrate the lady's reputation.

It was, John Mitchell who opened the interview with a formal request for full evidence disclosure. In other words, copies of any records or witness statements, or of course, any written record of complaint against his client.

The answer from Robert Snipe was fairly brief. "No". So, first blood to the opposition, or was it? Such a refusal to the solicitor's request could well have been interpreted as having been unreasonable, but the truth, as I was later to discover, was that there hadn't been any formal complaint made to police by the elderly Father Christmas, who was supposed to have bestowed gifts from heaven on the senior female cop.

In fact, John Mitchell did ask whether any formal complaint had been made.

The answer was as brief, if not different from the previous one.

"Yes," which at that time, was inaccurate.

Jean was suffering from a great deal of personal discomfort. Since having seen her home defiled earlier that morning by her junior officers, she'd been suffering from heavy menstruation, obviously triggered by the shock of the trauma she had been confronted with. By the time she had reached the interview room, Jean was suffering from the indignity of having blood run down her legs, and was compelled to ask, Malcolm Richards, if he could lend her ten pence to purchase a sanitary towel, not having any money with her.

Of course, he obliged the lady and then sat back and watched a junior male officer escort her to the toilet, creating further embarrassment for the female prisoner, as there was a legal requirement for only female officers to be present when escorting a female prisoner.

During the interviews that followed, there was a sense of immediacy with the same distasteful procedures being repeated on several occasions.

"Unbelievable," I gasped, trying hard to hide my true feelings of amazement behind a steaming hot mug of coffee.

Such incredible behaviour wasn't the main cause for concern that day. She was asked to sign various authorities to allow investigating officer's access into Bank and Building Society accounts in her name, which she agreed to do, not realising that two months previously, police had served writs on both Barclays Bank and the Woolwich Building Society. They had already completed financial examinations of every account held in her name. It was also later confirmed that the cops had been aware of the purported allegations made by, Arthur Grainger's family since August of that year. So why ask for signed authorities two months later?

In my view, there were only two reasons for such tactics. Either, these people were totally incompetent, or certain courses of action taken by them, were intended to create further stress or aggravation. I suspected the latter was the case. The kind of private person, Jean Goodman was known to be, would have been horrified by the thought of police officers' delving into her private financial affairs, as would have been the case I suggest, for most of us.

She found it difficult to recollect the majority of questions thrown hastily at her, remembering her solicitor insisted that she maintained her right of silence.

"Did you answer any of them?" I asked.

She nodded her head, explaining, "Most of them, but I just can't remember what was said. I was in a kind of dream. It was similar to having an out of body experience, as if I was looking down on the proceedings and wasn't actually taking part."

"I was silly. I remember them asking about three thousand pounds, Grainger was supposed to have given me and accused me of keeping, which was total fiction."

She stood up and left the kitchen, intending to search upstairs for a bank statement which would have proved her denial to be true, but I called her back, suggesting that it wasn't the time to start collecting evidence to support her innocence. That would come later.

"They kept asking about my relationship with, Arthur Grainger, and I remember telling them I had never had a relationship with the old man. That's all he was to me, an old man dying from Prostrate Cancer."

Jean then volunteered to tell me about the background to her association with her accusers, and how she had got to personally know Dora Winch and her father, Arthur Grainger, through her church, near to where she lived.

"I think it was in 1999 when I first met the old man, when he began to attend our church following the death of his wife. I had never met him or his wife prior to her death, but I remember his grand-daughter, used to occasionally turn up."

It was his daughter, Dora Winch, who had revealed that her father was suffering from the dreadful disease and was receiving hospital treatment.

"He always appeared to be tearful and was obviously still grieving the loss of his wife when he first began to come to our church. Anyway, during the two-year period after my initial meeting with him, my mother became extremely ill and most of my non-working time was spent nursing her at home. I lived alone with my mother, but Raymond used to occasionally visit and help out."

According to Jean, during that same period, the old man's daughter often visited and delivered gifts such as flowers, chocolates and cards, for her mother. She used to tell them they were presents of goodwill from her father.

"But, Arthur Grainger never personally entered my home during that or any other time," she told me.

"Did they know who you were, and what your position was?"

"Of course, everyone at our church knew."

She continued to explain about the occasion when, Arthur Grainger and his daughter, Dora, took a collection of bound books to church bearing the title, 'The Grainger Family'.

"Out of courtesy more than anything else, I agreed to read them and as a result, was then asked to study what I could only describe as a multitude of documents relating to their family history. In fairness I was briefly impressed by the detailed work contained in them, but if I was honest, they meant nothing really to me."

Jean stood and slowly walked across the tiled kitchen floor and gazed out of a window that overlooked the front of her house. Then she suddenly turned and looked directly at me, still grasping both hands together, as if tightly holding on to an invisible bell rope.

"Will I go to prison for this?" she asked.

Now I really felt some concern welling up inside.

"Who on earth gave you such an idea," I replied with obvious surprise.

"Malcolm reckons Snipe told him I might," She explained referring to her welfare representative, Malcolm Richards, "Apparently he said that I was likely to get five years for what I had done."

What could I say? If that had been suggested then there was a lot

More to this than the lady had been telling me. She certainly wouldn't be going to prison for having received gifts from an old man. I just shook my head and prompted her to continue.

"Eventually, Dora Winch told me her father had completed his own family history and asked if it was possible for him to research my own. Initially I was reluctant, having no real interest in the subject, but every time I met, Arthur Grainger in church he persisted, until I eventually agreed with his daughter for him to go ahead with his new project, which he referred to as 'The Jean Goodman Story'. Dora explained to me that it would provide her father with another interest."

"I considered such a project as being kind and considerate. He was an elderly gentleman who had no previous knowledge of my career details, so I was not unduly concerned. He mentioned at some time about putting my name forward for some national honour."

"Did you know he would have needed the Chief Constable's approval?"

"Of course, but I never thought it necessary to tell him. I didn't take him seriously."

Jean then made mention of a number of letters, Arthur Grainger sent to her, asking for her to amend certain items he'd written for the Jean Goodman Story. Her eyes lifted towards the ceiling, as she recalled ignoring them.

"I had other more important matters to deal with concerning the death of my mother, and looked upon anything, Grainger did as irrelevant. I believed it was all nonsense. None of it could have been taken seriously. I still can't believe this has happened to me."

She pondered for a moment and sat back down to take another sip of black coffee.

"Can you believe that? That's how much importance I attached to the man's ideas. And it was over the same weekend as my mother died."

I wondered what all this was to do with the allegations that she'd duped an old man into giving her gifts and put that question to her. The more I heard, the more puzzled I became.

"After my mother died, I continued going to church most Sunday mornings when my police duties allowed. Dora Winch often asked if I would talk to her father, as he had little to do with the other members of the congregation. I soon realised he was having difficulty in coping with his wife's death, so I used to pass the time of day with him, whenever possible, and always in church."

"Dora continued to deliver flowers and cards to my house and displayed a great deal of appreciation for the support I was giving to her father, although I didn't feel I was doing a great deal. They all appeared to become intensely involved in helping him with the Jean Goodman Story."

"Did you make any effort to stop all of this?" I asked.

"No. because I hadn't the time and in any case, I felt indifferent about what they were doing. I just thought it was a family doing their best to support their elderly father who was suffering from a terminal illness. I had no intentions of interfering."

"So, why didn't you just tell them how you felt?"

She looked hard into my eyes. "Would you have done so? As far as I was concerned this was an old man suffering from a terminal illness. When he began to pester me though, I became afraid to answer the phone. He was ringing constantly and I used to get, Raymond to pick it up in case it was the old man, but even he used to complain that I wasn't being very charitable towards him."

"How did he pester you, apart from being on the phone all the time?"

She sighed and sat back before answering. "I first began to encounter problems when I discovered he was visiting a local library for information relevant to my possible ancestry. He consistently telephoned me at home with questions concerning my own historical knowledge. Although he became a pest, I felt obliged as a practicing Christian to support him, and on several occasions, when I didn't want to speak to him, my brother had telephone conversations with him. Eventually even he began to get fed up with all."

"If it was getting all that bad, you must have done something, Jean."

"I mentioned my concerns about her father's obsessive behaviour to Dora Winch, but she dismissed them, explaining that her father had found a new purpose in life. On occasions when I visited church and her father wasn't there, she often said that he would be devastated by having missed me. I felt that such comments were harmless and without meaning."

"Did you explain all of this during the interviews yesterday?"

"I think I tried to. It all seems a blur. I remember telling them that during the four-year period I associated with the Grainger family at church, I actually gave, Arthur Grainger a lift either from his home to church or in the opposite direction on five occasions."

She frowned and placed a hand either side of her face. "That was it, Snipe suggested I'd manipulated the old man by giving him lifts to church every week. But that wasn't true. They were implying that I'd spent that time in the car, trying to con him."

"How can you prove that wasn't true?" I felt like a defence lawyer trying hard to prove my client innocent, but not really understanding what she was supposed to have done criminally wrong. I couldn't quite grasp what the cops gripe was about the gifts she was supposed to have taken from Grainger?

Finally, she admitted, "I can't."

"So, what about these gifts he's supposed to have handed over to you?"

"In April 2002 I had operations on both feet and was unable to drive or walk unaided for the next five months. I had to rely on crutches and was chauffeured to and from work by police drivers in official cars. I couldn't even go to church."

"During that period, I was immobile and cannot remember speaking to, Arthur Grainger or any of his family. I certainly didn't inform them that I was unable to walk unaided or drive a car. Only my closest friends and relatives were aware of that fact."

"I remember the old man telephoned my house several times during the time I was laid up but spoke to my brother. He began to leave small parcels outside my front door, each containing items of which I considered to be cheap jewellery. I arranged for, Raymond to return the items to him, but within a few days the same gifts re-appeared outside my front door."

"So, the gifts only appeared during a short period of time, April to October of that year?"

"Less than that."

"Why didn't you just tell him to sling his hook, because you were having problems getting about?" I was still playing Devil's Advocate.

"Because it was none of his business, and I didn't want everybody in the neighbourhood to know about the operations on my feet. I felt extremely indifferent towards the telephone calls from, Arthur Grainger and towards the gifts he left outside my house. I had recently lost my mother and was trying hard to come to terms with her death. I was also in constant pain and discomfort from the operations on my feet and wasn't at all impressed by the attentions of an old man."

"Eventually, it became obvious he wasn't going to accept the return of the gifts, so I decided to keep them in the parcels in which they'd been delivered, intending to return them to the, Grainger family through our local priest. My brother, Raymond agreed with that decision and offered to speak to the priest on my behalf. I was never given the chance because of what happened yesterday."

"Can you prove all of that?"

"I mentioned the gifts and what I intended to do, to various people. I can't remember at the moment, but I think I even told my hairdresser and a few of those at work."

"Did you tell the police yesterday?"

"Of course, I must have done. I just can't remember."

She was beginning to look more haggard and her words were becoming less coherent. I believed that rest was more important to her at that particular moment, than having the likes of me continue to probe her. So, I suggested to, Jean that perhaps I should leave her to take some respite and perhaps return later.

"Do you think I'm in a lot of trouble?" she suddenly asked, as I stood to leave.

She needed reassurance, but she also needed the truth and at first, I was reluctant to pass any verbal judgement on what had happened, without having first listened to the whole story. I stood for a moment, just staring into her tired eyes. She desperately needed to rest, but how could she with her mind so full of grief and terror. Finally, I quietly told her, "No, I don't think from what you have told me so far, you have a great deal to worry about. I know that's easier said than done at the moment, but I honestly believe that those who carted you off yesterday might have bigger problems to face in the future, than you have right now."

I sat back down and held both of her trembling hands in mine.

"Jean, there must be more to this than you've told me. I am finding it difficult to accept that your own Deputy Chief Constable would have sanctioned such dramatic and devastating action against you, unless there was more."

She just looked down at the table top and shook her head.

"Then there can be only one explanation. You are being set up, for whatever reason."

Chapter Five

Jean's brother was due to land at any moment, and it was obvious, his sister was fearful of being left alone in the same house in which her confidence shattering experience had taken place. She begged me to remain until, Raymond Goodman arrived, which I thought was only natural in the circumstances.

I nodded my acquiescence and returned to the stool in the kitchen, before continuing with a number of enquiries, which were still unclear. Being extremely suspicious by then, that there was most definitely some hidden agenda behind all of this, I asked, "Tell me what happened at the end of the interviews with Snipe and his crew."

"I've no idea of the time we finished. I was living out a nightmare. I remember being asked to sign some exhibits record which contained a pack of lies concerning a conversation I had with my brother, Raymond, when they were searching around this place. We'd been sitting side by side on the stairs when Ray had reminded me that I hadn't moved our mother's ornaments into the loft. They were piled up on the landing upstairs."

Again, she stood and walked over to the kitchen window, leaning against the stainless-steel sink unit. "It was an innocent remark, because they were cluttering up the landing space. Officers who had overheard our conversation wrongly assumed we were referring to the ornaments as gifts I had received from, Arthur Grainger. On my solicitor's advice, I wrote on the exhibits record what the conversation had been about and confirmed the ornaments belonged to my mother."

She turned and returned to her chair at the kitchen table and sat down, obviously trying hard to remove the mist that was still enveloping her memory.

"I remember, John Mitchell, asking for copies of the tapes of the interviews but was refused by Snipe. Both he and, Malcolm Richards told me they thought I was in no fit state to have been interrogated and would formally complain later. They took me up to my office on the seventh floor and searched that and my secretary's office."

"Did they recover anything from there?"

"I don't know. I don't know what there was for them to recover. It was all so embarrassing and demeaning. Snipe told me that I wasn't to have any contact with any other police officer, but the real shock came when he told me that I was not to visit my church, where my parents are buried. I can't even visit my parents' graves."

"He did what?"

"My solicitor objected but, Snipe just said that the order had come directly from, Adrian Plum, the Deputy Chief Constable. He added that if I felt the need to worship, I should find another church."

I had no doubt that the reasons for such a directive would have been feebly excused as a manoeuvre to safeguard potential witnesses but couldn't believe these people would inflict so much mental cruelty on one of their own, knowing that her life revolved around her job and her church. They had removed both, which strengthened my own resolve that there was a great deal of personal negativity involved.

"I think that, Bob Snipe was embarrassed by the order and left us for a time, saying that he wanted to telephone, Plum, to personally verify the instruction. When he came back he just confirmed that the order would not be rescinded."

Jean then continued to tell me that she thought she'd been released at 10.30 p.m. that night and had been taken home by Chief Superintendent Malcolm Richards. Throughout her ordeal, she had not been given a break or any refreshments, which was contrary to legal requirements. She'd been told to remain at home on the following Monday and await further instructions. But then more grief was about to come her way.

"When I arrived home, I remember I had an overwhelming feeling of shame, although I had done nothing wrong. I felt dirty, as if I'd been raped and immediately went upstairs to get a shower, and change as a result of my personal discomfort, and only then noticed a gold necklace belonging to my brother, was missing from a bedside table. I told, Malcolm Richards who said he'd make sure Superintendent Snipe was informed tomorrow morning."

"Are you sure about the necklace?"

"Yes, it was there before they came. They took it."

"Then might I suggest that you put your complaint in writing as soon as possible and give it to, Malcolm Richards to deliver to Snipe."

In view of the intruders' behaviour, I wasn't at all surprised that they would steal personal property from the house and told her so.

A faint smile came to her face and she nodded, before expressing another opinion. "I cannot believe that, Arthur Grainger has made a formal complaint about so much nonsense. I thought he was an honest man."

"Who's to say he's not," I answered, "Perhaps he hasn't made a complaint. This whole affair stinks to high heaven, but we need to find a motive behind what has happened to you. I cannot believe this has been done without something more sinister behind it all."

It was my turn to stand and visit the kitchen window. I allowed a few seconds of silence to pass by, before asking the inevitable question. "Tell me Jean, what was your relationship with, Adrian Plum, the Deputy Chief Constable, really like?"

She knew immediately what I was probing for, and answered calmly, "One of indifference."

Having listened to the complete story shared by, Jean Goodman, I was still finding it difficult to accept that police officers had acted in the way they had, without there being some hidden agenda I was not fully aware of. I was also finding it hard to believe that the lady's treatment and downfall was the result of some personal vendetta held against her by Adrian Plum, her Deputy Chief Constable, accepting that she had never alleged that was the case anyway. Even if there had been some professional friction between them, it still appeared to be ridiculous that someone would go to such extreme lengths as to deliberately destroy another officer's career, just because of some personal discord.

None of us had any real idea of what was going on in Jean's mind, or what psychological effect the trauma she had experienced, was having on her. During the week following her arrest and search of her home, Jean's brother, Raymond, kept me advised as to her state of health. From what he told me, it was obvious his sister's anxiety was increasing. However, there wasn't much anyone could do to help alleviate the gremlins busy challenging her sanity, until the next stage of the proceedings had been reached. That was to be a decision made by the Deputy Chief Constable as to whether or not she was to be suspended from duty. I was well aware, so were many others, that if such a drastic course of action was taken, it would place the lid on what had been one of the most eventful and successful careers ever known to the police service.

When a senior officer was suspended from duty, no matter what the outcome of any inquiry that might follow, the accused officer might just as well find a new career in Sing-Sing. There would be no turning the clock back. It would matter not, that the suspended officer was later cleared of all allegations. The Police Service as a whole had an historic culture of preferring the 'No smoke without fire' attitude, to reality. Such false perception was in most cases, encouraged and on occasions, fuelled by those ambitious individuals who couldn't give a damn about the effect such trauma might have on the recipient, as long as it offered an opportunity to leap into any senior vacancy that resulted. Such was the enormity of a senior officer's suspension.

During that particularly difficult period, Jean lived in hope that she would soon return to her post as Head of CID. I was less optimistic, although I didn't share my views with her. Having accepted there'd been no further allegations, in addition to what she had already told me, I remained completely discombobulated, and in some way, fearful for her future. It still didn't sit right with me. I suppose my biggest concern at that time of waiting to see if suspension would follow or not, was the way in which those individuals at the very top of her organisation, had allowed such serious misconduct committed by the arresting and search officers to actually take place. I couldn't help but feel there were those in positions of authority and power, hell bent on bringing her down, for whatever reasons they might have. The words, jealousy, chauvinism and perhaps even envy of her achievements in office, came to mind. But I also knew there would no way on earth, such intentions could ever be proved. One thing was certain, suspension from duty was the only way in which they could put the final nail in her coffin, no matter what followed afterwards.

During that same short period, I visited Jean on several occasions. Her real fear was that news of her demeanour would leak out, particularly to the media. She kept telling me that she could never face the public disgrace that would naturally follow. She was well aware of the existence of those in any police force who shared confidential stories with journalists, in return for payment of money, and she was also well aware there would be individuals who would have grasped any opportunity to have placed her in a bad light with the press. Particularly, those who she had transferred out of the CID during the purge she had previously maintained in an effort to rid the force of corruption.

Malcolm Richards made a number of representations to the Deputy Chief Constable, Adrian Plum, concerning the way in which activities during the search of her home and the interviews that followed, had been conducted. In fact, Malcolm raised a number of issues with the DCC, including the way in which the Inquiry had been directed in such a hostile manner, bearing in mind that the investigating officers were dealing with one of the most senior and indefatigable officers in their own force.

Although, Malcolm's impulses were laudable, his words and pleas were ignored. In response to his implorations, all he was told by the man in charge of discipline, was that the matter concerned a serious allegation, which needed to be treated in a serious manner, an opinion that most fair-minded people would have argued against.

Malcolm also asked why he hadn't been given any advance warning about what was to take place. As a Superintendent's Association representative and knowing that, Jean Goodman, would have been in need of legal representation, failure to notify, Malcolm Richards, was a breach of the agreement between his Association and the Association of Chief Police Officers.

He was stunned when Mr. Plum informed him that the matter needed to be kept, 'tight and confidential,' and that if Chief Superintendent Richards had been informed prior to the execution of the search warrant, it would have 'set the hares running'. If that wasn't a suavely intended challenge to a senior officer who had a well-earned force wide reputation for being the most trusting kid on the block, what was?

Malcom Richards also asked why the matter was being dealt with by, Jean Goodman's own force, and not investigating officers from another independent organisation. In reply, he was informed that, in Adrian Plum's view, there was no need. The DCC was concerned that if another force had conducted the Inquiry, details might have been leaked. I was astounded by the amount of bullshit that was being fed to the lady's welfare representative.

One other humane plea was made to Mr. Plum; to lift the ban on, Jean attending the church where her parent's graves were situated and was quickly rejected without plausible reason.

As far as my own position was concerned, I had given my oath to both, Jean and, Malcolm Richards, that I would remain discreet. None of what I had learned would be divulged to any of my contacts inside the media. The only problem I was having at that time was the vagueness of my own position and relationship with, Jean Goodman. I really had no idea why I was involved, except having offered an ear to an old friend and being capable from my own vast experience of investigative policing, to monitor what had taken place and advise on the best way to proceed further.

A time was eventually reached however, during that dreadful week of anxiety and almost unbearable apprehension, whilst awaiting helplessly, the decision as to suspension or otherwise, when Jean must have sensed my own feeling of insecurity. Would I be prepared to lead her defence strategy? This girl, although remaining extremely traumatised at that time, was still sufficiently clear headed to realise there was more than support of the propping up kind required. She was a fighter and knew that a professional investigator who had been responsible in the past for numerous and successful high-profile investigations into the most serious criminal offences, would be a good ally to have on side.

My first reaction was one of reluctance. I had my writing to consider, and other contractual commitments at that time, and I was in no doubt this particular case would be what we used to call a bloody good runner. It could very well be months if not years, before the whole matter was eventually sorted out.

Of course, the last impression I wanted to give was that I was playing hard to get, or short of the kind of commitment that would be necessary, never mind giving out all the wrong vibes regarding my belief in Jean's innocence. So, at first, I informed her that I needed just a little time to sort out a few ongoing things relevant to a book I was writing and would get back to her with my answer, as soon as I had reviewed my contractual obligations.

However, it was, Malcolm Richards, who I suppose finally twisted my arm, informing me that Jean would need all the professional help she could muster, if she was to avoid a blatant miscarriage of justice.

So, after a lengthy discussion with my literary agent, it was decided to put matters on hold for a short period. For now, it was sod my writing career, and to hell with those who were acting like covert Gestapo agents. What was quickly becoming a crusade, overshadowed by the personal affect the activities of the Special Projects Team were having on, Jean Goodman, urgently required a massive injection of optimism and motivation. Some kind of magical potion to replace the fear that was threatening to overcome her, instigated by a bunch of bully boys. So, it began, the fight back, but before the troops could be airlifted to the battle field, we all needed to know what exactly the strength of the opposition would be.

If she was suspended by the leader of the pack, then we would challenge vigorously, if it meant wading into the Home Secretary's Office one morning and kidnapping him. If the enemy continued to ignore her legal and human rights, again, we would challenge their callous audacity even if it meant soaring upwards to the Highest Court in the land to obtain legal remedy. And, most important, if they used the media to inflict more wounds on our client, then we'd do the same, only with the kind of transparency I knew the opposition wasn't capable of committing to. I was confident we could turn the tables, no matter what the cost.

But, we were still in there with a fighting chance without getting off our arses. The decision as to suspension still had to be made. Would common sense prevail and a ruling of no further action be made, or possibly the offer of advice as to her future conduct on the condition that, if she accepted such a course of action, she could return to her previous role as Detective Chief Superintendent. I told all of those involved, it was now all about staying low and waiting for that next step in what could very well end up with being a very dirty game of punching below the belt, already knowing the kind of individuals we would be dealing with.

Following her initial interviews on that fateful day, when her world was so cruelly shattered, arrangements had been made for Jean to be re-interviewed during the following week. When, Malcolm Richards called to tell her that those arrangements had been cancelled and put back a week, he also relayed his fears that the Deputy Chief Constable, Adrian Plum, might just be hell bent on suspending her from duty. After all, according to my own sources, he was the kind of diminutive man who, more than occasionally, liked to display his power and authority.

In response to that unwelcome prediction, she made an unusual offer, which even gave me more than just a flicker of optimism. She explained to, Malcolm that she was owed a total of no less than two hundred and forty-four days' time off in lieu and was prepared to take them if her continued presence in force would be embarrassing. Now, with the knowledge that such an offer could save the career of a senior detective, who could possibly turn it down?

One other issue that was evident at that time was the fact that the force had not offered any support with regard to their Detective Chief Superintendent's welfare. Of course, the Superintendent's Association hadn't been shy in stepping forward, in the guise of Malcolm Richards, but that wasn't the point. The lady's persecutors had a statutory duty of care towards all of its employees and, Jean Goodman was not an exception. Still, no support was offered, which was yet another hint of the existence of some conspiracy aimed towards driving her further away.

As the week passed by, John Mitchell, in his position as, Jean's solicitor, continued to demand from the force, full disclosure of the supposed evidence against his client, but was refused on each occasion.

Malcolm Richards continued to plead with, Adrian Plum, not to suspend Jean, but that decision was yet to be made, or so he was told, which only strengthened my own doubts. Finally, in the following week, just two days prior to the day she was due to be re-interviewed, Plum sent for Malcolm Richards

The Deputy Chief Constable told Jean's welfare representative that after much thought and advice from one other supposedly independent person, he had reached his decision. Detective Chief Superintendent Goodman was to be suspended from duty forthwith. Here ended the lesson in how to over react in a manner that was neither fair or equitable.

Chapter Six

The decision to suspend, Jean Goodman came as no surprise to some of us, although the lady's welfare representative found it difficult to accept. Malcolm Richards's initial reaction was one of disbelief, because of the domestic nature of the allegations made against her and knowing there had been no further inquiries made since his last meeting with, Adrian Plum. In fact, the circumstances and position of the investigation had not changed in any way during the period between the day on which the DCC had initially informed her representative that there were further inquiries to be made, and a week later, when he'd informed, Malcolm of his intention to suspend Goodman. But, according to Mr. Plum, his decision to suspend was 'in the public interest', which again was both bewildering and lacked justification.

Malcolm Richards obviously argued that was not the case and explained Jean's offer of taking more than six months off in time owing in lieu. However, Plum dug his heels in and declined the invitation, stating, "She has to be suspended." How uncaringly determined was that?

Malcolm was also concerned there had been other senior officers recently accused of more serious offences, including criminal deception, none of whom had been suspended from duty. He desperately pointed out that a second interview with Detective Chief Superintendent Goodman was due to take place in two days' time, and that the inquiries had yet to be completed. He suggested that the time to make such a dramatic and career destroying decision would be either, after all inquiries had been concluded or following a decision from the Crown Prosecutions Service concerning criminal conduct, which was the usual practice. He also indicated that another option would be to decide on her suspension, following any decision to either charge or summons the officer.

Plum told him that he felt he could not leave Jean at home, suffering from the misapprehension that she would not be suspended, and that following advice, he now knew she would be.

Malcolm directly asked who he had taken advice from, but the DCC refused to disclose that information.

Again, he implored, Adrian Plum to consider all of the circumstances, suggesting that suspension would not be proportionate to the allegations made against Jean, or the nature of the inquiries that would follow. Malcolm Richards also mentioned the need for confidentiality, suggesting that if, Jean Goodman was suspended, details would most certainly be leaked to the media, and she could be subjected to the most horrendous embarrassment and public disgrace.

All of the pleas made, were wasted words. None mattered, because Deputy Chief Constable Adrian Plum had shown the dissolute and incapacious side of his character, by his decision. The man was refusing to be moved. He called for Assistant Chief Constable, Anthony Freer, and explained that he wanted Chief Superintendent Richards to go to, Jean Goodman's home with Freer, who would then formally suspend her from duty.

Malcolm asked if he could have sight of the papers required for suspending a serving police officer, and Plum explained that there had not been sufficient time to complete them. "That will be done later," he confirmed, retaining an air of authority in his voice.

The Superintendent's Association representative explained, "At the time of suspending an officer, you must serve the appropriate documentation, outlining what that officer can do or not do."

Plum's only response was that, Richards should leave immediately with ACC Freer and suspend, Jean Goodman from duty. Again, Malcolm felt that, Adrian Plum's attitude was a continuation of the way in which the Inquiry had been conducted from the very start. He was of the view that it had been haphazard and obviously extremely over reactive. In fact, Malcolm Richards later stated that in his vast experience, both as a senior police officer and representative of the Superintendent's Association, he had never before known such a vast amount of focused energy, aimed towards bringing down an individual officer's career, either male or female.

Jean later received a telephone call from Malcolm, explaining the Deputy Chief Constable's decision. Her immediate response was one of shock and when I later discovered what had taken place, I then knew the gloves were off, and we were about to confront a powerful organisation that wasn't lacking in its sense of mental cruelty and arrogance. From that point on, we would all have one hell of a lot of work to do.

My own personal feelings were not important, although I did feel some anger when I first learned of this incompetent and unprofessional turn of events. If any doubts remained lingering in my thoughts concerning my involvement, they now disappeared beneath the thrust of, Adrian Plum's knife into my friend's heart. My new-found role was to remain objective, as I had done so when managing so many major investigations when serving as a Detective Superintendent. I was determined to run the whole defence Inquiry in the same manner as when I relied on Major Incident Rooms, only now, I wouldn't be looking for an individual perpetrator of a murder or other serious crime. I would be taking on the police service in the knowledge, that this institution was now a mere shadow of that which I had served with respect, commitment and dedication.

Even before, Jean Goodman, had been formally suspended from duty, I had recruited a small gathering of the finest retired detectives the police service had ever known, with a sprinkling of serving and well trusted individuals who would be my ears, passing on any useful news from within the organisation which was hounding her. I couldn't tell my new-found club members what exactly their tasks would be, or even the real purpose for me calling on them. That would come later. Firstly, my intention was to assess the opposition, and find out exactly what was really behind what I then felt was nothing more than a charade.

Later, that same evening both, Malcolm Richards and Assistant Chief Constable Anthony Freer, landed at Jean's home address. Freer appeared to be confused and a little embarrassed at the obvious urgency of the task he had been given, but both officers were invited inside.

The Assistant Chief Constable formally told. Jean of, Adrian Plum's decision, and she asked if it would be alright to record the proceedings on an audio tape. The senior officer agreed. What followed was a further breach of procedures laid down to protect officers suspended from duty.

The fact that the appropriate documents, which are supposed to explain to an officer why they are being suspended and what rights they have, were not served on her at that time, actually resulted in the suspension being improper and invalid. What did strike home to those involved was that, here was a highly successful police officer with more than thirty years unblemished service, who had to listen to an Assistant Chief Constable spurting out details which all told the same story. Her career had formally been brought to an abrupt end, no matter how unfair or how unjust.

Although the lady appeared dazed by what she was being told, ACC Freer continued with his effort to explain what, Plum had told him to say. That the matter would remain discreet, and that those officers involved in the Inquiry had been made to sign silence agreements. When they left, Malcolm Richards wasn't sure whether, Jean had actually heard a word that had been spoken inside a house which had the potential of becoming her tomb.

Now then, discretion and confidentiality were words thrown about by the official side, like chaff in a wheat field. And yet, within a few hours of. Jean Goodman's suspension, on the following morning, a popular local newspaper carried a front-page article containing details of Detective Chief Superintendent Goodman's suspension from duty, with a full-blown portrait of the lady herself. Discretion and confidentiality had just been ignored, in a similar manner to Jean's legal and human rights.

Prior to that first edition of the newspaper hitting the streets, an old mate and top crime reporter at the paper, telephoned to ask if I knew anything about the Goodman case.

"Where did the story come from?" I enquired.

"You know I can't say that," he quickly answered, "But it was from a good source, a woman who works in Police Headquarters. Not too distant from the top of the tree over there."

Well, that was enough for me. 'Not too distant from the top of the tree' meant only one thing. The very people who had orchestrated the lady's downfall were now responsible for making sure she would suffer the indignity of seeing her career wrecked, publicly. What a great bunch of smarmy bastards. The enemy had shown no mercy in delivering her unfortunate circumstances into the hands of the general public.

I was almost apoplectic and broke every speed limit to make Jean's house that same morning. Malcolm Richards was already in situ by the time I arrived. It was time to truly take stock and put all of our experiences and policing knowledge into a strategy that would turn the tables on those who had drawn first blood. After all, by using the media in the way they had, they were defining the battle ground, which it just so happened was my home territory.

Those last few days towards the end of October and beginning of November 2002, must have been the wettest ever recorded. It never seemed to stop raining and I remember the wiper blades on my old Mondeo, struggling to keep the windscreen clear on one particular black night, when I was slowly making my way down the M.6 from Manchester. Fortunately, I was walking back to my car, having grabbed a quick bite from one of those service stations which usually charged enough to require a second mortgage, when my old friend the farmyard cockerel suddenly croaked. It was my daughter, Jo.

"Dad," she said in an excited voice, "A reporter has just called at the house asking questions about, Jean Goodman."

"Where is he now?" I asked, diving into the car to shelter from the cascading waterfall crashing down from above.

"I've told him you're not here, so he went away, but he's sitting outside the front of the house in a car."

Could you believe it? I had suddenly become a target for the national press. I didn't know whether to feel proud or angry. I felt angry and told my daughter not to worry and that I'd be home very soon.

When I finally arrived outside my house, there he was. A dark figure, sitting at the steering wheel, without any lights showing, like a common burglar running his eyes over potential targets. At first, I was tempted to just walk over and punch him on the nose for having bothered my family. But there again, he was probably just some kid trying hard to do his job, having been sent to my residence by some jumped up editor back in some dry and warm newspaper office. So, I parked up and stood in the pouring rain, waiting patiently for some nervous youngster to come shuffling over towards me, triggering a security light at the side of my house. At least I could see his face now.

At the time, I was still writing my weekly feature for a local paper, and hadn't given much thought up until then, how I should approach my own editor regarding, Jean Goodman's circumstances. I was confident they wouldn't have printed anything without her consent, but the time would come when the situation would need to be addressed. But that was a few days away, so what did this young feller want from me?

I didn't catch his name; being too busy holding a copy of that morning's Manchester Herald over the top of my head. He told me he worked for the Daily Express and I quickly corrected him, asking what news agency employed him.

His brief smile was illuminated by the security light, as we both stood facing each other, in the kind of weather that should have been giving farmers some concerns. And any poor sod living near a river, if it came to that.

He confirmed the name of the agency which employed him, and continued, "The Daily Express has asked us to verify a story regarding Detective Chief Superintendent Goodman's suspension."

I laughed. Well it was better than just unleashing a string of metaphors before racing for the safety of my home.

"How the bloody hell can I verify any story concerning, Jean Goodman?" I asked, "If I knew of any story don't you think I would be telling my own newspaper, pal?"

"But it's about you, John."

That cancelled out any thoughts of dinking this guy and escaping through my own back gate.

"Come again?"

"There's an unconfirmed rumour coming from London that you and, Jean Goodman have been business partners, and you're now being investigated by the cops. Do you want to make any comment?"

Well now, if Old Nick himself had suddenly appeared at that very moment and breathed fire between the cheeks of my arse, I wouldn't have flinched an eyelid. Knowing such a ludicrous suggestion had to be denied, to prevent tomorrow's editions carrying that particular piece of libellous garbage all over the front pages, I made an immediate decision to put the lad right. The only problem which rapidly ran through the analytical channels of my mind, was that just a denial would probably not suffice. The nationals would need more, but not before I'd teased this kid for just a few seconds longer.

"It's bollocks," I said, not trying to be over subtle you understand, "It's got nothing to do with me or any bad business transactions undertaken by, Jean Goodman."

"Come on John," he pleaded, "I've been waiting outside here for the past couple of hours. I can't just go back with a denial, you know that."

I've always been a softie at heart, except when some scumbag had just knocked over some old lady's handbag or smacked a sixty-year old security guard in the mouth with the butt of a sawn-off shotgun. And the kid was still only trying his best to do his job, so I gave him an accentuated account, as best I could.

"Look," I said, trying to sound sincere, "It's about a few domestic allegations connected with a member of the public and nothing to do with her job as a copper."

"An illicit love affair?" he asked in hope.

"No, sorry. More of a load of old cobblers that I don't think for a minute will see the light of day, once the old bill has got it sorted out." I placed a hand on his soaking wet shoulder. "Trust me and tell your gaffers that in a few days time, it won't make the sports pages."

"I need some more," he demanded.

Now the persistent little shit was beginning to get up my back.

"You're not getting anymore, because she's asked me to help her out with this one, and that kind of compromises me. She's been accused of a load of dribble concerning a member of the public, and that's all I'm going to tell you."

The lad's head dropped, so I placed an arm around his shoulder and casually escorted him back to his car, in similar fashion to having just found some long-lost orphan.

"Listen," I said, sounding more paternal towards him, than a fellow journalist, "What I've just told you is more than anybody else in the media is aware of, and that to my mind is an exclusive. Cheer up and be glad of small mercy's."

At least he seemed to brighten up a bit and bade me a pleasant farewell, before driving away to share his new-found storyline. The only problem now, I realised, was that the dogs of war would be all out to discover the whole story behind the lady's suspension, and she had to be warned.

Well, they came from all directions. Don't ask me how they found out her home address, except I suppose we could have thanked the good old police service who had already broken God knows how many promises to keep Jean's suspension out of the media. But the press had never been shy in obtaining whatever information they had needed to progress the makings of a juicy story.

During the next few days, there must have been a reporter from every national newspaper in the country, land at Jean's front door. Of course, by the time they did show up, I'd already warned her and suggested she didn't open the door or speak to any of them. It wasn't the time to court the media. Her employees had already done that, and I knew we had to tread carefully, until we, or perhaps I should say, I, was aware of everything there was to know about the allegations made against, Jean Goodman. If only that crop of weirdos would fulfil their legal obligations and provide us with evidence disclosure, but according to John Mitchell, they were still obstinately digging in.

Chapter Seven

None of us were entirely happy about the manner in which, Jean Goodman had been suspended, but there were more important issues for us to tackle. I called the first meeting of those few individuals I had recruited to assist in, what was to be the subsequent inquisition. We needed to find out the reasons behind a charade, which I was convinced, was a front to conceal something far more serious and perhaps sinister, behind destroying the lady's career.

It was early days and I intended approaching more selected professional detectives, as our enquiries expanded further, but for now, three retired former colleagues met me in a small city centre bar, which we knew was not frequented by police officers.

Andy Greatrix was a former Detective Sergeant, who had earned a reputation for a vast number of successful convictions resulting from his outstanding commitment and persistence in investigating some of the most heinous crimes imaginable. The tall, lanky individual, who was completely bald with a thin moustache across his upper lip was certainly no male model, but rather a black country, down to earth man, who had never let me down in the past, even when tasked with some of the most tedious jobs. Andy had the patience of Jove, which would be an asset should the journey we were about to undertake, become tedious and drawn out.

Neil Rowbotham had been another gifted and highly skilled detective, who was an expert at delving into suspects backgrounds and habits. What other investigators failed to pick up when making routine enquiries, Neil, another former Detective Sergeant, could unravel from a vast array of contacts he knew in all walks of life. On a number of previous occasions, even I had been surprised at the speed in which the man, with short fair hair and a flushed smiling face, had put together a full dossier of intelligence on an individual we had been looking at.

The third member of the team was a retired Detective Constable by the name of Sandra Jenson, a single but still attractive lady, whose analytical skills were second to none. If there was ever a person I needed to turn to, who could read someone else's mind and forecast an individual's actions, Sandra was the lady and had often displayed on many previous occasions a character that was fearless and highly responsible.

All three retired detectives had been a huge part of my own successes in the past. Each and every one of them was mature, dedicated and trustworthy, as they had proved when dealing with a vast number of incidents when serving both Queen and country.

After our initial welcomes and enthusiastic exchanges of updated, personal news, I wasted little time in explaining the reason I had requested their assistance. My old comrades were unanimous in agreeing to be part of the investigative team I was putting together, and accepted without question, the cause we were about to embark on, was morally right. I couldn't help but compare this particular trio with those who had been part of the bullying tactics used prior to, and following the arrest of Jean Goodman, and it felt good to once again, be in the company of true professionals.

There was much to do, and the first major enquiry I needed to be completed concerned the Grainger family. Those who, according to Superintendent Snipe, had instigated the complaints and allegations made against the now suspended, Head of CID. I needed to know everything there was to know about those people, least of all the background and motivation of, Arthur Grainger. I found it difficult to accept that an eighty-six-year-old man would have played a leading role in bringing down, Jean Goodman, and suggested my small team of specialists concentrated on all the members of the old man's family. It was a starting point from which we could launch our Inquiry, and my intentions were to run our investigation in similar fashion to how we had dealt with, far more serious crimes in the past.

Contact numbers were exchanged and we all agreed to meet at the same location on future occasions, whenever there was a need. At that point, secrecy was an essential ingredient to potential success, but my former associates were already fully aware of that factor.

The next commitment on my agenda was to meet up with, Malcolm Richards, and shortly after that first meeting with the operational team, we shook hands in that same, safe inner-city location. Between us, we quickly ascertained that we shared the same concerns regarding the true reasons behind the way in which the female Detective Chief Superintendent had been treated, and both agreed that a crude form of victimisation existed.

One other concern which was mutual, was our suspicion that, because of the disproportionate manner in which, Jean had been treated, compared to the minor allegations made against her, was it possible there did exist some other, more serious malpractice she was suspected of having committed? The disproportionality I was referring to, was just too unbelievable to be accepted.

Malcolm agreed, but also pointed out that, if such a hidden agenda of a criminal nature did exist, then surely it would have been revealed in support of having suspended her. We agreed, we could only play the game with the cards dealt to us, but that wouldn't prevent us from treading cautiously, especially during the initial stages of the procedural stages that were to follow.

It was also accepted by the pair of us, that Malcolm would concentrate on Jean's welfare, which was his official position, leaving myself to focus entirely on delving into more operational matters, which

I was beginning to relish more as the days passed by. We would still work together and perhaps confide more when our different areas of responsibility became linked. One important part of our strategy was to be transparent. I strongly believed, that Jean Goodman's dilemma had resulted from a witch hunt, without justification, so every enquiry we made, and every step we took, would be done in an honest and open environment. Such agreed philosophy was soon to be tested.

You can imagine my delight when my team of specialist detectives came back with what I could only describe as, stunning and jaw-dropping news. In just two days since being allotted their first major task, they had delved and probed into the Grainger family's activities in recent years, and the results were far more interesting than I could ever have imagined.

It transpired that, over a five-year period, Jean Goodman had been the third high-profile public figure, against whom, Dora Winch, Arthur Grainger's daughter, had made outrageous, career destroying allegations. The previous two victims had included a renowned solicitor, who the woman had complained had been responsible for raping her.

The second claim made on behalf of, Arthur Grainger, had suggested that a highly placed cleric and member of the Church of England, had been involved in attempting to defraud the old man of thousands of pounds of cash. Neither allegation was evidenced or proved to contain the slightest hint of truth, and both had been eventually dismissed without any further action having been taken. In fact, the lawyer, who had been traced and interviewed by, Andy Greatrix, had told the former detective he had actually considered taking legal action against, Dora Winch, but having realised the allegation made against him was so preposterous, as to be detrimental to his character, decided against such a course of action.

A brief file containing the full details of the historical misdemeanours committed by the, Grainger family, was quickly compiled and sent to, Detective Superintendent Robert Snipe at Police Headquarters. I also included my own observations, which suggested the previous behaviour of, Dora Winch, negated any credibility which might have been contained in the allegations made against, Jean Goodman. I suggested that the suspension of the female Head of CID should be immediately lifted, and that the lady should be restored to her former position without further delay. A copy of the same intelligence file was also sent to, John Mitchell, Jean's solicitor, who was based in Bristol.

There was no celebration; we were far too professional to bestow any form of congratulation on each other. Yet, I could not see any reason why we shouldn't quickly be notified that Jean's case was to be reviewed. That was the least we could expect in the circumstances. How wrong was I?

There was no acknowledgement from the police of them having received the result of our enquiries; no recognition of a possible serious error having been made, and certainly no acceptance that the Special Projects Team had been used for whatever sinister motive lay behind the course of action taken against Chief Superintendent Goodman. To say we were all mystified by the lack of any positive response by the cops, is an understatement, and even more puzzling was my own attempts to make follow-up calls to both Superintendents Grossman and Snipe being blocked. In fact, contrary to what we had been anticipating, the force which had been served so professionally and innovatively by, Jean Goodman, decided to go down another, different path, which I found to be distasteful and shockingly inept.

Two weeks had gone by since our lady's suspension, during which time I had surreptitiously increased my team of specialists, with a couple of trusting serving detectives who had agreed to assist our cause. This particular pair had served with me on various crime squads and were both officers in whom I placed the highest level of trust.

The news of the manner in which the police had responded to our attempts to restore, Jean back to her former position, came as a devastating blow. A decision had been made by the Deputy Chief Constable to subject both myself and Jean, to surveillance operations. Such enterprises also included the placement of intrusions on our home and mobile phones. What were these people all about?

Of course, initially I hit the roof. Instead of facing up to their legal requirements and responsibilities to seek out evidence to prove the innocence of the woman they had subjected to such neglectful and irresponsible trauma, they had decided to follow us, dressed like scarecrows or street lamp posts. Why? I had to ask myself. For what purpose? Tapping our phones was a serious and accountable course of action, never mind the cost in man power to perform such practices. But again, why and what could they possibly hope to achieve? They were not investigating a suspected serial killer, or Islamic Terrorist. According to their own admissions, they were in fact, concentrating on Miss Goodman, only because some prat had suggested the Head of CID had conned an old man out of a few gifts. Even if it had been true, and that was looking extremely doubtful as each day passed by, surely the cops were persisting in going over the top, just a bit.

The information given to me by one of my most reliable sources, was so unbelievable, I just had to put the potential reality of such practices to the test. So, I deliberately phoned, Jean on her mobile and arranged to meet her at a local railway station, near to where she lived, later that same afternoon.

It had been a few days since I had last set eyes on the lady, and when I turned up for that meeting, I was greeted by a pathetic looking female figure, dressed in an olive-green mackintosh over an old jumper and pair of slacks; she appeared to have the weight of the world on her narrow shoulders. I also noticed how, Jean's eyes appeared so lifeless, as if she really had no idea of where she was.

I had already approached the young man in the ticket office at the station, who I had got to know fairly well over the years, when using my preferred mode of travel, and asked if he would let me know should any strange face ask him the location of my intended travel. As soon as I suggested that the strange faces might belong to cops, his eyes brightened, and I just knew I could rely on him. The constant odour of burning cannabis in the background, was also an excellent beacon to confirm that when it came down to getting one over the cops, he would be first in the queue.

"They've tapped our phones and put surveillance on us," I whispered to, Jean, "So, we need to buy a few new chips for our mobile phones." She just stared back at me, with expressionless eyes, and still apparently pondering a future life in space travel.

To emphasise my point, I then explained that our own team of supporters wouldn't be able to converse without being overheard by the law, and half the bloody police force would know in advance, our every move.

She must have understood because a frown appeared on her bewildered face.

"They wouldn't do that," she suggested.

"Lady," I said, "Trust me, they're pulling out all the stops to land their biggest fish. Now, unless you haven't yet told me about your plan to assassinate Tony Blair or his missus, it means the people who are hounding you are worried. That means, they've realised what they've done already is a load of bollocks, and I suspect they're now looking beyond the original complaints against you, to justify the cock ups they've already made. Does that make sense?"

She just smiled and nodded her head. Her whole demeanour was similar to a child just learning to cross the road safely, and if I had been in possession of a bag of jelly babies, I would have given her one.

There was one other person standing nearby, on the normally quiet, open-air platform. A bloke in his mid-thirties dressed in a dark open necked shirt and pullover to match. He'd appeared at the same time as I caught my first sight of the train approaching from some distance away. Surveillance cop? Of course. It was written all over his forehead, so I bided my time and waited until the train had come to a standstill and the yellow light, which tells you it's time to press the button which opened the doors, was illuminated.

With Jean standing close behind me, I reached out a hand to press the door button, quickly looking to my left, where our escort was going through the same hand movement. I then quickly withdrew my arm and guess what? He did the same.

I must admit to treating the episode with some flippancy, as I laughed out loud, enough for him to hear, and then opened the door and climbed inside. We didn't see him again during the journey into the big city, but in fairness to him, we weren't supposed to, the gent being a surveillance dick and all.

Anyway, during the trip, I quietly explained in more detail how we would purchase enough phone chips and would later explain the reasons why, to the rest of the crew working with us. I told, Jean of our utmost need to remain vigilante. It would be a waste of money, if having bought half a dozen replacement chips for our own and the team's mobiles, the coppers then discovered the details. It would be a futile exercise because all they would have to do was to tune into the new phone chips, and they'd be back in business.

She told me about a telephone call she'd received from an Acting Assistant Chief Constable, Henry Gunnell, on the morning following the press release concerning her suspension. Apparently, Henry, who had also been a former boss of mine and a man I'd admired for his forthrightness and transparency, had been asked to be her contact with the force. The problem with that was, old Henry Gunnell was due to retire from the force within a couple of weeks. That didn't say much for, Adrian Plum's alleged care and understanding of his top detective's situation.

Anyway, Gunnell had phoned to give her a roasting about the press coverage, suggesting that if she leaked any more information to the press she would have to suffer the consequences. That didn't say much for the Acting ACC's welfare skills or tenacity. It didn't say much for his knowledge of what was going on either, otherwise he would have known the story released to the press, came from the same floor he worked on at Police Headquarters, and not from, Jean Goodman. In any case, why the bloody hell should she feel it necessary to inform the media that she had been suspended from duty, only to wreak havoc upon herself? Non-the-less, it eventually transpired that was the last time her only official welfare contact with the force would ever speak to her.

But now, it was time to spring the trap I had set, as we climbed down from the train, after arriving in the city centre. I looked for the man we had exposed when first catching the train, but there was no sign of him. It didn't matter; I knew only too well, there'd be another half a dozen surveillance cops supporting him, or I had completely misread the situation. There was no way we could go anywhere near a Vodafone shop with a bunch of official onlookers on our tail, so I had to be sure whether our predicament was safe or otherwise.

Chapter Eight

We walked through the railway station complex, arm in arm, heading towards a convenient exit which would lead us to the main shopping complex. We didn't rush and just paced ourselves in the normal manner, not having gone far before my suspicions were confirmed. There he was, pretending to converse down a mobile phone, just in front of us, and in the shadows of a large ornamental Victorian drinking fountain, which had remained dry for as long as I could remember. It certainly wasn't the best position for a covert officer to take up, and if any of my operatives performing in another life, had put themselves in such an exposed location, my boot would have sent them flying.

As we walked past the pretender, I wished him a Merry Christmas, and suggested he waited where he was, because we would be returning that way in about half an hour. He ignored me and continued whispering down his mouthpiece. Well, so what? I couldn't resist taking the piss out of these reprobates, knowing how much of the public purse they were wasting.

Another bright-eyed kid stopped just in front of us to light a cigarette, obviously waiting for us to walk past, so he could follow from behind. It was all so amateurish as far as I was concerned, but decided to play their game, although I was becoming more doubtful about covertly obtaining any mobile phone chip replacements on that particular visit to the shops. I think the fact I'd spent my hard-earned cash on a couple of train tickets and didn't want to waste them, stopped me from turning us both around and making our way back home. Also, because I wasn't treating 'Operation Playtime' with any genuine seriousness or respect, I decided the real litmus paper test would come inside the mobile phone shop, so continued on our short journey.

It was Jean who first noticed a couple of kids standing behind me, as I waited in a short queue at the Vodafone service counter. She had recently re-joined the living and stood back by the door, as alert now, as I was. It was obvious she hadn't been noticed as they came in, obviously to get close enough to see what I was up to. When she heard them talking in riddles, she fronted them and just stared into the eyes of both operatives. I turned to see the anger in her eyes, but before I could grab each of them by their throats, they turned and bolted back out of the door.

"We can't do this," she whispered.

"I know," I said, "I'll just have to think of some other way to get those phone connections changed."

Jean wanted to get something from a shop just around the corner from the Vodaphone store, so I suggested I would wait for her in the same location we'd just been visiting. I knew she was finding it difficult to go anywhere alone but had my reasons for wanting her out of the way, even for a couple of minutes.

As soon as she'd disappeared from sight, I casually stepped across to the opposite side of the street and approached a tall, thin lad with fair hair. The kid was wearing that many ear rings, I was amazed he wasn't standing there, lob sided. He'd never taken his eyes off us since leaving the railway station, and I knew from past experience, he would have been the main eyeball, directing the surveillance operation during that part of our journey.

I was angry about having been treated like some common criminal, but also well in control. I just stood facing him for a few seconds, watching his eyes roll in every direction, but straight ahead.

You see these kids are taught to look straight into a target's face, whenever the geezer they're doing a number on, stares back at them. It's supposed to be a natural display of ordinary human behaviour, although I've always had my doubts about that one. Anyway, what they find difficult to do, is to eyeball a target who has the audacity to stand just a few inches away from their nose, showering them with plenty of non-verbal communication.

He coughed nervously, and I pushed him back into the same recess of the shop doorway he'd been occupying since we had first disappeared inside the Vodafone shop, opposite.

"I want the name of the force written across your warrant card pal, or your bollocks will leap out of their sack," I explained, with more than just a little hostility in my threat. After all, I was not in the mood at that particular time to befriend any of these people.

"GMP," he replied instantly, obviously recognising a pair of eyes filled with real intent, leaving him in no doubt the level of his voice was about to reach a much higher crescendo. He'd made a good guess, but his answer puzzled me. Now I knew that the hierarchy in Jean's force, had really gone over the top, deploying a surveillance team from Greater Manchester Police. I had my doubts about what the officer with the ear rings had just told me but didn't want to take it any further. Besides, I did wonder just how expensive this business was becoming and what the public would think of their money being spent in such a crazy and unnecessary manner. Perhaps someone, somewhere had reckoned on, Jean being the Head Poncho of a nest of professional assassins, or if it came to that, perhaps yours truly, was suspected of planning a seditious move against the Queen.

"Call it off," I suggested, "You really ain't that good at it."

He smirked, probably hoping I'd dink him and then he and his cavalry could have carried me off for good. But I wasn't there to drop in the shit, and just turned and walked away.

They were still there, all the way home on the train, and I was already scheming how I would obtain a change of phone chips without leaving my home address. It didn't take long for that to happen, with a little help from other trusted people who were sympathetic towards our cause. Very soon after that escorted trip into the city centre, everybody was soon back in protected covert communication with each other, including lawyers, detectives and of course, my good self.

It later transpired that the kid in the shop doorway had told me a 'porky'. The surveillance team had been obtained, not from Greater Manchester, but from a neighbouring force, which was later confirmed by that force's Head of CID, who was also a close ally of, Jean Goodman's.

We also became aware later, that, not only had they tried to shadow, Jean for at least a couple of weeks during that time period, but static observations had been maintained on her home address by police officers armed with a video camera. The authorities for the surveillance operations had been signed by the Deputy Chief Constable, Adrian Plum, and the reasons given were later found to be astonishing. But that comes later. There were other important matters to be addressed first, such as obtaining further evidence to support the truth about the false allegations which had led to her downfall.

It was during the week following the surveillance exercise, when Jean's brother, Raymond, telephoned me concerning a near disaster. He'd found his sister, sitting alone at the same kitchen table, around which she'd previously briefed me on events prior to her suspension. The table top was covered with tablets of all shapes and sizes, neatly stacked up in front of her bowed head. But the alarming item was a note addressed to him, explaining the reasons why she had taken her own life.

When I arrived at the house, I found both sister and brother still sitting in the kitchen. The tablets and personal note of intention had been removed, but from the lady's appearance, I had no doubt her intention to commit suicide was real enough. Jean's haunting eyes were encircled with black rings; her face was pale and drawn, but the most defining sign of severe distress was contained in her facial expression, which resembled a featureless Plaster of Paris mould. I was looking directly at a waxwork figure of the woman I had previously known.

There was no time to lose, as far as I could make out, and immediately told Jean's brother to drive her to their local surgery. It was more than just concern bothering me. I genuinely feared for the lady's sanity and life.

When Doctor Lisa Barratt, Jean's local General Practitioner, heard of the reasons for her patient's attendance, she immediately closed her surgery and spent most of the remainder of that day concentrating on the distressed woman's mental instability. She counselled her in some depth, offering tremendous support and reasons for optimism. She went beyond her calling as a medical practitioner and befriended her stricken patient, inputting all that had been missing from Jean's life, since her traumatic ordeals. Medication alone was insufficient, and Doctor Barratt made arrangements for the disturbed senior detective to see a psychiatric nurse, who also eventually became a close friend and confidante. Between them, those two professional women helped to restore, Jean Goodman to a level of acceptable behaviour and stability, and she would forever be in their debt.

Acting on the doctor's advice, her brother remained with her at home, following the day spent at the surgery. When I visited Jean the following morning, she was still tearful, but at least looked a lot better, and less out of touch with what was going on in her life. I suggested we went for a drive and she agreed. Having said that, she was still not back to her usual self and perhaps never would be. Each time I spoke to her, I was looking into a pair of expressionless eyes, in a similar way to how you would expect a person under heavy sedation to appear but knowing that wasn't the case with this particular lady.

"Where are we going?" she asked quietly.

"You'll see," I replied with a confident smile.

I drove into an inner-city district; a slum area in which, Jean and her brothers and sister had been born and raised. She said nothing as she stepped from the car and stood staring at the front door of the small terraced house in which she had lived out most of her childhood. The house was one of a line which faced an opposite row of small terraced homes, divided by small gardens and an access path running down the centre.

"This is where life really began for you," I suggested.

She nodded and began to indicate locations in the vicinity where various incidents had taken place, some funny, some tragic. She remembered the way in which her parents had struggled to keep going, having to feed four hungry mouths, and the tears flowed freely down her face.

I could only hope that what I was doing, was the right course of action to take. It was a gamble, but one I was prepared to take, confident a trip down memory lane might hopefully restore some of her confidence and strength. I felt there was a need for, Jean to remember her humble beginnings, before then concentrating on all that she had achieved, and I think it worked. Well, that was until we stepped across to the end of the narrow cul-de-sac, which overlooked a canal.

"Did you ever play as a kid down there?" I genuinely asked.

Jean shook her head, as we both stood on a narrow footbridge crossing the canal.

"No," she quietly said, looking down into the cold and black water, "That's where my great grandmother committed suicide."

For a moment there was a pregnant pause of silence between us.

"Oops," I said, "Never mind."

We then both burst out laughing at my clumsy attempt to bring nothing but happy memories back to her. But at least her humour had returned.

On the car journey back, we talked about the need to face up to life's crises, and how we should always find the strength with which to carry on. I had been brought up in a similar environment to Jean, and used my own experiences to convince her that, we from the backstreets were made of stronger material than most.

On occasions she laughed, she also cried, but during most of the journey home, her resilience returned by the bucketful. By the time we arrived back at her house, I knew that some of the old, Jean Goodman had been restored. The same, Jean Goodman who had dealt with numerous minefields of male domination with her head held high. The same, Jean Goodman who had fought her way to the very top of her profession, without turning a hair or being influenced by fools. The same, Jean Goodman who had achieved what most men could not. Take the Criminal Investigation Department by the throat and clean it up.

"The ball is in their court at present," I tried to explain, referring to the internal investigation that was supposed to be ongoing. "But your turn will come, and then you will have your day, rest assured."

"Can you promise me that?" she asked humbly.

"Yes, I can," I answered truthfully.

Malcolm Richards called with news that was a little less dramatic. Obviously by then, we had been made aware that the second interview the cops wished to conduct had been cancelled, and Malcolm was still waiting for a new date to be set. However, in response to formal complaints made by Chief Superintendent Richards, concerning the inept way in which, Jean had supposedly been suspended, arrangements had been made for the appointment of an over-viewing officer, Commander

Richard Ferguson, from London. Arrangements had been made for the new guy on the block to meet Jean on neutral ground, at a local hotel. It was intended to serve formal notices on her and of course, attempt to formally suspend her from duty, yet once again.

She went with, Malcolm Richards to the Regency Hotel, where she met Commander Ferguson, who was accompanied by a Chief Superintendent. Documents referred to as Regulation Nine Notices, which outlined the allegations made against her, all concerning the acceptance of gifts from one eighty-six-year-old, Arthur Grainger, were duly served – finally.

Assistant Chief Constable Anthony Freer, the officer who had made such a cock-up of the initial attempt to suspend Jean, was also in attendance, and once again, attempted to formally suspend her from duty, although he still had problems observing the required procedures by failing to inform her verbally of a few domestic matters, concerning loss of expenses and other ancillary issues affected by her suspension. But not to worry, as she later said. He did his best.

The real shock came, when Superintendent Robert Snipe also turned up, a man who, Jean now believed was a major player for the enemy and possessed a truculent streak, which could only be to her detriment.

Commander Ferguson tried to explain to both Jean and Malcolm, that Snipe was only there to assist a smooth take-over of the Inquiry. They were both right to view such an explanation with suspicion, because it later transpired that Robert Snipe actually remained the Senior

Investigating Officer.

No member of Jean Goodman's team ever clapped eyes on Commander Ferguson again, following that initial meeting. It was all so cosmetic. A deliberate ploy to conceal whatever injustice and abuse that still existed beneath the surface, and an attempt to cover their backs. Anyway, before they all departed to go on their merry ways, Jean and Malcolm were told that arrangements were being made for her to be re-interviewed in a month's time. And of course, pigs can truly fly.

During the days that followed, Malcolm Richards persisted with his representations to have the ban lifted on Jean attending her church and visiting her parent's graves, but his pleas still fell on stony ground. He also continued on numerous occasions to make requests to Superintendent Snipe, for full disclosure of the alleged evidence against Jean but was repeatedly denied. I could only assume that the reason for such refusals were because there wasn't any evidence to disclose. I was convinced more than ever by then, that a witch hunt aimed towards finding something from the lady's past to use against her, was the reality of why she was being kept in total isolation.

From my own sources, I also discovered that close colleagues and friends had been directed not to make any contact with the suspended woman, adding support to another notion I had, that there was a deliberate strategy being operated to add as much grief and mental anguish to the suspended officer, as possible. I genuinely feared that it was all a deliberate attempt to either, force, Jean Goodman to take her own life, or take voluntary retirement.

On a more positive side of this manipulated siege situation, was the lady's mail box. During the few weeks following the first press announcement of her suspension, the newspaper which had carried the initial story, received no fewer than two thousand letters of support from members of the public. Every missive was forwarded to, Jean, and I for one was extremely grateful to the editor. We were all taken aback by some of the kindest and appreciative comments and remarks contained in the dispatches, imaginable. They certainly helped to lift some of the gloom from the lady's shoulders.

As the days and weeks flew past, Jean continued with her psychiatric counselling sessions, interrupted by the occasional visit to see Doctor Barratt. There was no further news regarding the date of a second interview and with Christmas rapidly approaching, her solicitor, John Mitchell obtained a full statement of evidence from Jean's local priest, in which he confirmed she had made a number of important comments to him regarding, Arthur Grainger's attentions towards her, and the gifts she was hoping to eventually return to the old man's family. In similar fashion to the evidential file relevant to that same family's dubious historical activities, the statement from the priest was forwarded to Superintendent Snipe, but alas, was ignored.

My own personal involvement was committed to my team of investigators who had by the end of the year, sifted out some incredible evidence, which not only supported, Jean Goodman's non-culpability but supplied a reasonable motive behind the allegations concocted against her.

However, following the Christmas break, we were all subjected to an unexpected shock which totally pulverised everyone who had been working so hard to prove, Jean's innocence. Personally, I did not believe she had any case to answer and was still trying hard to identify any criminal act she might have committed. I was guilty of having completely underestimated the determination of the enemy, when, Malcolm Richards visited to confirm to Jean, the Crown Prosecution Service had directed that there was sufficient evidence to prosecute the former Head of CID for charges of Fraud, and that she would be summoned to appear before the courts in due course. Obviously, the person who had instigated all of this, had powerful and influential connections that reached far and wide. I was stunned and mystified by this new revelation.

Chapter Nine

My career in journalism had only just began and having been extremely fortunate to have been allocated a feature page by my newspaper editor, I felt a little exposed and perhaps ungrateful, having devoted so much time to, Jean Goodman's case. When I was summoned to the editor's office, I knew exactly what the problem would be.

Dave Collins was an old hand in the newspaper business and before taking on the role of editor, had worked at various levels for both the national and local press. The tall, well-built man with a full beard and wide girth was sitting behind his desk when I entered the office, and the first thing I noticed was boxes of sausages stacked up in one corner.

In answer to my quizzical look, he told me that the family run sausage business I had written an article on the week before, had been so pleased with my comments, they had actually delivered twenty-five boxes to the newspaper offices as a gift to show their appreciation. And why not bestow plaudits where they were deserved. The proud company had been the most efficiently run I had ever come across, and their products were certainly way beyond any competitive challenges.

I smiled, knowing there would soon be one hell of a lot of reporters putting on weight very quickly, not least of all, the editor himself.

"But that's not the reason why I wanted to see you," he quickly confirmed, "Your feature for this week's edition on the increasing volume of transport on our streets, isn't quite up to your usual standard."

"I apologise," I immediately replied, "And I know I haven't given it the same attention as usual."

"Quite frankly, I found it to be boring, and I'm sure our readers would have felt the same."

Dave Collins was nothing like the kind of newspaper editor the majority of people tend to conjure up as an image of what a newspaper editor is like. Some geezer who runs around with a cigar in his mouth, dressed in an open necked shirt beneath a black waistcoat, bawling and shouting at everyone within striking distance. In fact, he was quite the opposite; quietly spoken, analytical and on occasions philosophical. He was an honest individual who called a spade, a spade, and had little time for flowering things up. He usually left that to his many sub-editors.

I had already temporarily severed my book writing commitments with my agent, and the last thing I wanted to do, was lose my position with the paper. So, I decided to be truthful and fall on my own sword if that was an accurate description of what was about to happen. I told him of my involvement in the, Jean Goodman case, and the fact that I truly believed the lady was being set up for reasons, which had not yet become clear.

Dave nodded his understanding, obviously already having an inkling of the reason why I hadn't been turning up so full of enthusiasm, as was the usual case.

"How long do you expect to be involved in all of this?" he asked, bluntly.

"For as long as it takes," I confidently, but also apologetically answered.

"Until you clear the lady's name. Is that it?"

"Until I unravel whatever is really behind the way in which she's been treated by her own organisation, or rather, by a few highly powered individuals, who call themselves senior investigators."

The editor stood and stepped across to a metal cabinet adjacent to his window, and after pulling open a drawer, took a copy of the sister newspaper which had publicised the initial story relating to, Jean Goodman's suspension. He stood for a short while, scanning over the leading front-page story, before commenting.

"It says here, she was suspended in relation to matters of a domestic nature, not connected with her work in the force. Why is that?"

"Why is what?"

"How come they decided to suspend her, if their enquiries were not involving allegations concerning her police work?"

I briefly gave Dave an attenuated account of what had taken place, including much of the information I had gleaned in favour of the former Detective Chief Superintendent, and which supported her innocence.

He turned and looked directly at me with a suspicious eye, and then remarked, "Again, why on earth would they suspend such a high-ranking officer, as Jean Goodman, for such a trivial allegation?"

"That's the question I intend to find the answer to, by making what enquiries are necessary."

The editor returned to his seat, and leant back in his wide chair, explaining, "I understand she is going to court for this?"

"Yes, that seems to be the case."

"Okay, I'm hooked, so tell me, what kind of person is she?"

I described, Jean as being highly principled, honest and totally dedicated to her job. In the four years she had been in post, the lady had rid her department of a number of idle and untrustworthy individuals who had just been turning up to work for years, just to collect their wages.

"Therefore, it seems obvious, she's made a few enemies during her time at the top of the tree."

I knew what Dave was getting at, and put forward my own opinion, based on my experience as a former top detective.

"That may be so, Dave, but the circumstances of what has happened to her, are different to it being the result of some vendetta. I can't help but wonder if she's been at the receiving end of some orchestrated plan to get rid of her. Some kind of conspiracy fuelled by some threat or risk she represents to some high-flying individual or possibly, even a group of them."

"If that's the case, and I trust your judgement implicitly, perhaps we can help her."

I was all ears, and remained standing there, wondering what sort of notion had been concocted in the man's mind.

"Accepting that there has been a miscarriage of justice in this instance, or there is likely to be one if she is ever convicted, we will support her, at the same time condemning the actions of those who are persecuting Miss Goodman."

"In return for, what?" I asked.

"Her full and exclusive story at the end of it all."

That was the icing on the cake as far as the paper was concerned, and although the offer of support was most welcome, I could envisage a problem.

"You do realise that, if she gets through this successfully, as a serving officer, she wouldn't be allowed to disclose anything to the press."

"Of course, but I wasn't thinking of a feature written by, Jean Goodman, rather one written by yourself, containing all the detailed information you have. Of course, I would have to run it past the lawyers before going to press, but I can't see any difficulty there."

I didn't need any time to think about the offer. Dave Collins idea was brilliant, but could only come to fruition provided, Jean was acquitted at court. Having witnessed at first hand, the kind of determination shown by the police to get rid of the lady, I had doubts as to just how far they were prepared to go, to ensure she went to prison, which would mean another overdose of pills coming to the fore.

After accepting my editor's offer and promising to pay more attention to the next series of features I had planned for the newspaper, I left, feeling a little confused as to the direction in which we should be going next. The boxes of sausages remained where they were, and I never, ever, had so much as a sausage sandwich from them.

We met in the usual place in the city centre, and at my request, the original three members of the team were joined by three more. Now there were seven of us in total, all specialised former detectives, street wise, self-motivated and familiar with each other, all having worked together at various stages of our careers, mostly on crime squads and when investigating major crimes. It was a small battalion of dedicated people who always looked under the bucket as well as inside it.

Dave Stewart was a stocky individual, who had a reputation for being a bit of a prankster. However, he was trustworthy and reliable. He also had a habit of being in the front line, when things got tough.

Paul Lownie had been widely known by his nick-name, 'The Hooded Claw', because of his quiet manner and habit of disappearing from the operational theatre for, on occasions, a number of days, only to return to the fold with sufficient intelligence or evidence to bring a complex investigation to a speedy conclusion. No other detective had anywhere near the number of informants as Paul often utilised.

The sixth member of the team, excluding myself, was, Roland Guthrie, a former undercover officer who had been involved in some of the most perilous situations, befriending individuals suspected of being involved in heavy crime. Rolly, as he was known to those who knew him, was fearless and his acting abilities would certainly have been given credence at the Old Vic.

But there was also a seventh member of my team of highly trained investigators, who was known only to myself. An unusual man who was still a serving detective, and who I hoped would be my personal Ace in the Hole. But he had been put on hold, until the time came when I would require his services.

I discussed splitting the team into three sections, two operatives working on each section, in similar fashion to how we had co-operated so effectively on previous occasions. The sections were to comprise of, intelligence gathering, operational commitments, and analysis. It would be the responsibility of those committed to operations to converse with contacts they personally knew were serving officers; examining what documents they thought might be important to the case and piecing together, snippets of important information they could glean, before passing the same to the officers designated to the intelligence section.

The latter would collate whatever raw information was passed on to them, with a view to transforming material into intelligence by corroboration and confirming the accuracy of the information. Further enquiries might be necessary to achieve that aim, and it would be their responsibility to do just that.

Finally, the two people given the job of analysis, would be tasked with evaluating that which was passed to them from the intelligence duo, and basically sorting the wheat from the chaff. They would also be required to identify and link any separate pieces of information that might be connected with each other.

So, there we had it. Each member of the team was given each other's contact mobile numbers, which were guaranteed to be beyond the knowledge of the police. The whole set-up had been fashioned on previous successful strategies, and every one of them knew exactly what was expected of them. I knew that, no matter how long it took to achieve our ultimate aim, there would be no malingerers; no lack of, or dilution of enthusiasm, and certainly nothing spoken outside the boundary lines of the team.

"What if, Jean Goodman is convicted?" Dave Stewart asked, "Where would that leave us?"

"Working harder than before to get her released," I answered, "But be prepared for the long haul with this one, as I have every reason to believe she will shortly be serving a term in the jug."

"What makes you say that, if you're convinced she's innocent?"

Sandra Jenson enquired, with a look of surprise.

"Because of the type of people who are dealing with her, and the same individuals we will be looking at."

After buying a round of drinks, I then took them through the nitty gritty of what our next move would be. I explained that I required half the team to dig into the backgrounds of the leading members of the opposition, namely, Adrian Plum the DCC, Robert Snipe the officer in charge, and a Commander Richard Ferguson, an officer from the Metropolitan Police Force, to see in particular whether the man had any links with Plum or Snipe, or any other officer based locally.

The other half of the team were given the task of researching recent cases in which, Jean Goodman had been involved.

"We are looking for any incident that could have implicated any other senior officer, over the past couple of years," I explained, "Anything, no matter how trivial, that might be construed as being detrimental to anyone else working with Jean. Concentrate on senior officers and not the rank and file people."

It was similar to turning the clock back a few years, and I could sense already, a growing atmosphere of camaraderie amongst them, which shouldn't have been any surprise, considering it felt as though the last time we worked together, was the day before.

Finally, we were about to strike back at the opposition. What had been a testing time, waiting for various decisions to be made by those investigating, Jean, had come to an end. Now it was our turn, and I had every confidence that the investigative quality of my own people would eventually unravel whatever truth was being concealed behind such a chauvinistic display of blatant cruelty.

At least, whilst we were all challenging our wits against the opposition, Jean Goodman would be well out of it; reading through those letters of support sent in by the public. That could only be good; in fact, very good.

Chapter Ten

Patch Humpage was a sort of human anecdote for anyone who wanted to test their sense of smell. If someone couldn't pick up his scent before actually laying eyes on him, they were either suffering from a bout of influenza or had their nasals completely blocked. Patch didn't just live in the backstreet gutters, he represented them, having been one of my most effective undercover officers during the days I was serving. He was what was often referred to as, a deep cover operative, but I had often wondered whether the lad remembered the true nature of his employment, or just preferred his way of life to that which was awaiting his return back to the rank and file. In fact, I often wondered if anyone knew he was still a serving cop, or even whether he was still alive and kicking.

The six-foot, blonde haired lad, with the pale face and drooping eyes had just about experienced every kind of perilous situation imaginable, when working in the darker side of life. The problem had always been that, Patch was the best at his undercover job, and being the best meant very little rest or respite for the enthusiast, being sent on one undercover job after another, most of them being in other force areas either in the North or South of England. So, when he telephoned to suggest we meet, it was a feat accompli, as I had already been tinkering with the notion of recruiting his services to the current campaign.

"I see you've still got that complex about soap and water," I remarked, wrinkling my nose as I approached the bar he was leaning against, in a narrow backstreet public house, familiar to both us from previous meetings. Where else would be more suitable for crossing paths with such an individual, than right bang in the centre of the red-light district, where every next-door neighbour was a criminal. It was a safe enough place though, for people minding their own business, and which most cops regarded as off limits. It also brokered little interference when we discussed matters not for anyone else's ears, particularly relating to some seedy undercover job, with which, Patch was in need of some help or support.

Nothing much had changed about the place. There were a couple of local nondescripts sitting on benches that ran around the perimeter of the room, trying hard to make a pint of ale last until closing time, and obvious contenders to challenge my old mate for the title of who went the longest without addressing their personal hygiene. Although most of the interior was in permanent shadow, the bar itself was quite well lit up, and Patch was standing in his usual spot at the end of the bar, furthest away from the door through which I had made my entrance.

We shook hands and I gratefully accepted the undercover detective's offer of a drink, before pulling up a stool to face him more directly. The lad with the shoulder length, straggly hair and knotted beard, was never one to mince his words, and got straight to the reason why he'd dragged me away from the comforts and safety of the countryside in which I lived.

"They've made a right balls up of the Goodman case," he said in a whisper. "Everybody's been told to stay away from her, no phone calls or anything."

"Aren't they supposed to be allowed to phone her occasionally, if only for welfare reasons?" I asked in reply, knowing that the correct answer should have been in the affirmative.

Patch shook his head, "No, they're out to break her by keeping her in isolation. It just ain't right and some of us have cut up, but we've been told that if they find out we've phoned her, our necks would be on the line."

One thing about this particular piece of reliable news was, at least it confirmed that there existed an ongoing attempt to break Jean, in whatever cruel and harsh way they meant to achieve it. But the question as to why, remained a mystery, and I was hoping that my former operative could provide the reason.

Patch continued, "I've got a good source working on the Professional Standards Team. She wasn't around when they turned Ma'am Goodman's house over but has since been given the job of looking into her background, to see if they can come up with something nasty to throw into the equation."

"How trustworthy is she, your source?" I asked rather naively, before taking a gulp of lager from a pint glass which appeared to be covered in a year's grime and stuck to my fingers when I lifted it up from the bar, in similar fashion to how my feet had felt as though they'd been glued to the floor matting, as I had earlier stepped across from the entrance door.

"It's not about how trustworthy she is, it's about how trustworthy I am. The girl's risking a lot just talking to me."

I nodded in agreement. "Why do you think they're going to all this trouble, Patch?"

"No idea," he said shaking his head with a slight smile on his face, which was a rarity for this particular undercover officer, "I guess they are just trying to save face, having already thrown her to the wolves. Anyway," he continued, leaning towards me, heaven forbid, "That dipstick, Snipe, has threatened other senior detectives not to make contact with her and they're going to bring in a full isolation policy, supported by those numbskulls in Special Branch. But it's that little turd, Mr. A Plum, who's apparently behind it all." He was obviously referring to the Deputy Chief Constable, which seemed strange that a man in such a high position would be so vindictive. The more I learned, the more I was becoming convinced that there was something personal involved in the whole shoddy affair.

"I think they've already done that mate."

He nodded, before enquiring if he could be of any further help, so I made my feelings known to him.

"I'm convinced something really seedy is behind all of this, Patch, and I suspect that, Jean Goodman is a main player, without realising it." I paused, as he took another drink, before wiping his mouth with the back of his grubby hand.

"Could your source try and find out for us?"

"I doubt that, she's not high enough up the ladder to be in a position to probe that deeply."

"Then might I ask that you sniff around a bit more and try and dig up any information linking a senior officer with the underworld. If what we are faced with is something of a criminal nature, then there has to be some villain involved somewhere."

"Not unless, whoever is holding a vendetta against the lady, is a lone wolf."

I nodded my acceptance of that possibility, and conceded that such a theory was possible, but we had to find out and the only way we could do that was by keep digging and looking at all possibilities. At first, I was reluctant to pass on my new mobile number to him, but then realised that Patch Humpage was probably the most trustworthy man I had ever known in my life, so gave it to him.

"Give me a bell, Patch, if anything turns up."

It was his turn to nod, and after leaving him, I had a strange feeling that what we were putting together was a formidable armada of expert detectives, which now covered most investigative fields. My mind continued to dwell on the basic problems we were now facing. I had always been the kind of bloke to follow my heart rather than what was going on inside my head, always teaching my younger detectives to look under the bucket instead of just inside, and to expect pink elephants to come flying overhead at any given time. In other words, when investigating a crime, imagination can be just as useful as forensic science. As far as the legal part of my thinking was concerned, even if, Jean Goodman had willingly accepted those so-called gifts from a pensioner or admirer, she hadn't committed any crime. And yet the lady had been subjected to the most horrendous treatment inside her own home; she'd been suspended from duty, deliberately knowing that would end her career, and was now evidently being kept in isolation from her force, just to drive the nails home.

The latest revelation concerning the decision to put her before the courts, was in my view, yet another attempt to push her further towards the brink of insanity. There was no other logical reason for such a course of action, and if that was the case, then there must have existed some powerful persuasion being bestowed upon the Crown Prosecutions Service, which could have only come from a high-ranking officer, possibly the Deputy Chief Constable himself. No, I couldn't accept that was all as a result of accepting a few gifts from an admirer. Okay, she hadn't informed the Chief Constable of old, Arthur Grainger's attentions, but in usual circumstances, such an oversight would have been worthy only of advice.

There was of course, one other avenue of logical thinking. It was feasible that whoever had first triggered the start of this Inquiry into, Goodman, had overshot his or her boundary lines, and having now realised the enormous amount of incompetency which had engulfed those initial enquiries, was trying hard to introduce something else that might have taken place in the past. Some minor misdemeanour committed by Jean, perhaps when she held a lower rank, but which if discovered would help justify their actions thus far. That was certainly a favourable option and knowing what kind of conceited individuals could be found occupying the highest of ranks, it was quite possible. By sacrificing an individual just to save face, was highly likely. One thing was certain, knowing the lady as well as I did, all the delving into her past record would, I was convinced, reveal nothing untoward. My mind continued to leap from one theory to the next, without coming up with any positive answers.

Within a couple of days, two of my team, Sandra Jensen and Roland Guthrie came back to me. Both had been given the intelligence roles and were requesting a meet to brief me on what they had unravelled so far.

"It makes interesting reading," Rolly Guthrie explained, referring to a notebook he'd made up, "And we are only going back a few months."

"Okay," I said, "I'm all ears."

"It appears that earlier this year, Jean Goodman challenged a number of the force's surveillance unit, having found out they had been fiddling their expenses."

"How?"

"It seems that there was an existing practice whereby times of occurrences had been changed in the official notebooks of officers engaged on various operations," he quickly explained, "The purpose was to record that individuals had been on duty, when in fact they hadn't, the purpose being to claim overtime, which hadn't in fact been worked."

I nodded my simple understanding but remained unconvinced such a discovery would produce the kind of determined vengeance we were looking at.

"But there is a knock-on effect from such a corrupt practice," Sandra Jenson went on to explain, "Those same officers had previously been involved in serious crime cases, and in which they had been required to give evidence at court. One of those instances involved the murder of a police officer, Gabriel Thorne."

I remembered that particular case where a patrolling policeman had been shot dead in the street, having walked into an armed altercation between two rival gang factions. I also knew instantly where my two people were coming from.

"And, what you are saying is that, if surveillance officers were falsely cooking the books, it was possible they could also have given false testimony during that trial."

"Yes, but not just that one trial," Rolly continued, "Imagine if such corrupt practices became public, the fuss defence teams representing convicted individuals from various trials which had involved evidence being given by those same bent officers, could make in an effort to get successful appeals against conviction."

"Murderers, armed robbers and a posse of other serious miscreants, all walking free," I suggested.

They both nodded.

"Not only did she discover that notebooks had been altered," Sandra explained, "But according to the reports, Jean Goodman submitted to the Deputy Chief Constable, evidence to show that overtime logs had also been falsified and entered for payment."

I sat back, totally flabbergasted by the realisation that what, Jean had unearthed, could have had devastating effects on the force as a whole. Individuals who had been given life sentences could be set free. The cost involved in having to review and disclose to the Judiciary what had taken place, would crack the budget wide open, in addition to the public embarrassment the force would be subjected to, which would also be colossal.

"There's more," Rolly Guthrie continued.

I looked at him, completely bewildered.

"Just prior to the raid on, Jean Goodman's house, when she was arrested, we found a record of a meeting which had taken place between herself, the Deputy Chief Constable, the Head of Special Branch and, Abraham Long, the force solicitor. Miss Goodman's concerns were raised, but we couldn't find any outcome from that meeting, and as far as we know, the matter remains unresolved."

That was it. Such a turn of events was dynamite and had all the ingredients of having been the reason for such determination to remove, Jean Goodman from her post. If such a revelation ever became public, heads would be put on the block, including, Adrian Plum's.

I congratulated my two on the work they had done, and agreed with them, that there was every likelihood their initiative had provided a number of answers to most of the problems we had been facing. And yet, there still remained in my mind, some doubt as to whether such circumstances would have fitted the bill. Perhaps I was being too sceptical. We needed to keep the information, Sandra and Rolly had uncovered, covert for the time being, until I had been given the chance to consider what our next move would be. One thing was certain; there was every possibility the circumstances might be leaked to the press, in the same way as, Jean's suspension had been. A few bloody heads would be chopped off then.

Chapter Eleven

Although, when I next visited Jean, I was still feeling vexed by the manner in which we had been subjected to surveillance, she was looking a lot stronger and what pleased me more, was the fact she might be up to providing further information, in particular concerning her most recent work, before being arrested. I urgently needed to discuss the problems she'd been having with the Surveillance Team's expenses but recognised a need to progress cautiously.

Once the tea had been poured, we both sat in her lounge, reminiscing about times gone by. It was a deliberate ploy to measure just how much she had recovered. The realisation of the decision made by the Crown Prosecution Service to put her on trial, was obviously more than disappointing, and in the lady's case, she appeared to be holding it all together a lot better now.

We talked about a few incidents we had shared in our younger days, working together, and Jean even managed to chuckle at some of the more humorous activities we got up to. Finally, I was relieved by the way in which she seemed to have recovered, if not fully. So, decided to mention the discovery she had made concerning the corrupt practices of her surveillance team, earlier that year.

"I had forgotten all about that," she confessed, with more enthusiasm in her voice than I had heard since that dreadful day when she was taken away from her home, "How could I have forgotten?"

"It's understandable," I suggested, "Considering what you have gone through." I then reiterated what my two operatives had discovered, and she quickly agreed their account was accurate.

"If such practices had been made public, there was a real chance that a large number of killers and other serious offenders would have been set free by the Court of Appeal," she confessed.

"What were your feelings about that possibility at the time?" I asked, taking a few sips of my tea from a Denby china mug.

"The same as I believe is the case now. That there was only one direction to take, and that was to be open about it. Failure to bring matters out into the open then, apart from being construed as interfering with the course of justice, could only have caused greater damage to the reputation of the police service later. I firmly believed that."

"And you made that suggestion to, Adrian Plum and the others who knew of the details?"

"Yes, but apart from the DCC the only others who had been made aware of what had been going on, was the force lawyer, Abe Long and, Clive Hipkiss, the Head of Special Branch. But I recall also suggesting that before deciding to go public, we needed to instigate a thorough internal investigation into the complete activities of the Surveillance Facility, over recent years, so we had the fullest picture."

"Can you remember the responses from the others at that meeting?"

"Of course, it was only a few months ago, and Adrian Plum in particular, strongly favoured we should let sleeping dogs lie, which I was astounded by. Those were his exact words."

"And how did the other two react to that suggestion?"

She paused to think, and then answered, "Abe Long kept his own counsel, and Hipkiss agreed with the DCC, which was no surprise, as he was Plum's lap dog and would never go against his leader's ideas."

"So, as far as you know, nothing was done about what had taken place, the reason being that a situation whereby individuals convicted of notorious crimes, could possibly be released, had to be avoided."

"As far as I know, yes."

I stood and carried my empty mug into the kitchen, at the same time, calling back to the lady of the house, "Tell me, Jean, do you think it's possible they were worried about the risk of you leaking the details of what could have been disastrous to the force, and that's what this has been all about?"

"It's possible, yes," she called back.

"If your career hadn't been so quickly and cruelly brought to a standstill, would you have parted with the information publicly, even without the DCCs agreement?"

"No, not at that time. As I've already said, I felt there was a need to investigate the matter further. We needed clarification and to learn the facts, before taking any action. But I do recollect now that I suggested the Chief should be made aware as soon as possible."

"How long after that meeting had taken place was it, before you were arrested?"

"Just a couple of weeks."

"And have you any idea whether the Chief Constable was made aware of the circumstances?"

"No, I've no idea, but knowing the devious way in which, Adrian Plum operated, I very much doubt it."

On the face of it, such preferred antics by the Deputy Chief Constable certainly appeared to be sufficient to try and neutralise, their Head of CID, if he thought for one minute she was a threat to the reputation of the force being dragged through the gutter. And yet, was it the kind of problem, you would go to all that trouble to conspire with others to bring her down? There did appear to exist a pervading sense of misguided loyalty towards, Adrian Plum, and I wondered what kind of decadent existence he led. We didn't really know enough about the man.

As I drove across town to the television studios, I considered further the implications that could have evolved from a group of officers, having been found to practice fraudulent claims, after giving evidence on oath in various major trials. I agreed wholeheartedly with, Jean's opinion that such circumstances should have been subjected to an in-depth internal Inquiry. But there again, if I was genuinely concerned that my Head of CID was likely to make such a potentially catastrophic situation public, why not just move her away from Headquarters, into a post distanced from the investigative arena. After all, by taking the course of action they had chosen, would that not heighten the risk that she would inform the press of such far reaching malpractice, in any case?

The other small matter was, if the situation concerning the corrupt practices of the Surveillance Unit was the motivating factor behind what had happened to Jean, where was the connection with the Grainger family, who had conveniently come on to the scene, apparently at the right time. Unless of course, that had been purely co-incidental, and the powers that be, had grabbed the opportunity to exaggerate what was in reality a load of rubbish. Finally, I concluded to myself that the whole affair should be shelved, temporarily, or until we had more definitive evidence showing that it was undoubtedly the motive behind what had taken place. We had to concentrate on our primary objective and not be deflected by whatever red herrings were thrown at us. Those could be scrutinised at a later time.

Bill Graveney was the local Home Affairs Correspondent for the BBC and a friend I had known for many years prior to the, Jean Goodman Inquiry. In fact, Bill had reported on several occasions, the progress of Jean's case, or lack of it. Although, what little I had seen of his news reports to camera, they had always appeared, in my view, to have been fairly accurate and well balanced, which was an opinion I was soon to discover, wasn't shared by the police.

At the television journalist's invitation, I met him in a balcony bar, come restaurant, adjacent to the studio complex. Bill was an impressive looking man, tall with dark brown hair and always smartly dressed as a result of the requirements of his occupation. He had a reputation throughout the region for being meticulous about his work and had brought home to the local BBC news programmes, many exclusive stories.

"Did you see my piece last week on the Jean Goodman's case?" he asked, slouching back in one of a number of soft armchairs which were positioned around small tables, there for the use of visiting diners. The menu could wait. It was obvious that something had rattled my old friend's cage.

I answered in the affirmative, stating that I thought his series of short news items had been extremely pointed but truthful. In fact, the correspondent had made a number of statements which suggested that the Goodman Inquiry was being conducted in an unfair and unjust manner. So, I wasn't completely surprised when he told me that the police had formally complained to his boss's in London.

He produced a copy of an email which had been sent by the force's press office to the Board of Directors at the BBC in Wood Lane, London. The message basically accused, Bill Graveney of trying to disrupt an ongoing police inquiry, and showing bias against the investigating officers, that could be construed as being obstructive and detrimental to the proceedings. The electronic missive also contained allegations that the reporter had publicly made a number of inaccurate statements, including one suggestion that, Jean Goodman had been made the subject of surveillance.

"I was given some information from a reliable and well tested source that the force had kept her under surveillance after suspending her from duty, so included that in my report. But now, the board is hounding me and telling me to stop this absurd badgering of the police service. I feel like some delinquent in danger of being thrown off his hobby horse."

"You were right to do so," I assured him, still scanning down the list of alleged discrepancies in front of me. "Take it from me, she was the subject of surveillance, in addition to having had her phone tapped."

He was obviously relieved, but some concern remained in his eyes.

"I've also been targeted by them."

"You, but why? How could they justify that?"

"How can they justify anything they've done so far?" I then went on to describe the events of that Saturday afternoon, when we had both been followed into the city centre, by a team claiming to have been seconded from Greater Manchester Police.

"Furthermore," I said, "These so-called inaccuracies which were contained in your report are all true, and I can produce evidence to prove that they are, especially relevant to the surveillance fiasco."

Bill's eyes lit up, and he asked the obvious question, "How can you do that?"

"By handing over documentary evidence, which will support the claims you have made."

What Bill wasn't aware of, and if it came to that, neither was, Jean Goodman, was that one of my team, Dave Stewart, had actually got his hands on a copy of the authorisation instructing the surveillance team to focus on both myself and, Jean. According to Dave, the record had been signed by, Adrian Plum.

"Would you do that?"

"Of course, but I haven't got what you need here with me now, but it shouldn't take long to get it across to you. On top of that, be my guest if you feel a need to disclose the evidence to your board of directors. The only thing I ask is that you return the documents to me and treat them as being highly confidential. You could use a copy of the signed authority for the surveillance on, Jean Goodman, but I have to insist the remainder of the documentation stays out of the public eye for now." The cops had blatantly denied the existence of any surveillance on, Jean, so I thought it would be in the BBC's best interest to broadcast evidence showing the way in which the police had attempted to mislead the broadcaster.

During those earlier weeks, and with some help from my team, between us we had managed to compile quite a dossier of evidential information, the majority of which consisted of various documents which had negated much of what was contained in the allegations against Jean. Most of that which had come into our possession had been forwarded to, Robert Snipe and the Special Projects Team but much to my disappointment, nothing had been done. Potential witnesses whose identities had been disclosed, had not been interviewed by police, and our efforts had been met with obvious apathy.

The following day, I once again met up with, Bill Graveney, in a restaurant just outside Stratford upon Avon, where I handed to him the dossier of evidence we had compiled, including the copy of the authorisation bearing, Adrian Plum's signature. It provided the journalist with empirical evidence to show that both myself and, Jean Goodman had been subjected to round the clock surveillance. It would also go a long way towards convincing his bosses that his previous reports had been truthful, and that if anyone had been lying, it was the police.

The reasons contained in the record for the authorisation of the surveillance, were outlined as follows;

To confirm, Jean Goodman's home address and personal movements.

To confirm that, Jean Goodman was in fact living in the UK.

To confirm that, Jean Goodman had other male friends in addition to Arthur Grainger.

It was an extraordinary and implausible list and, after reading through it, Bill smiled and said, "I wouldn't have believed this, unless I had seen it with my own eyes." He was astounded, and yet I remained indifferent, having already witnessed at first hand, just how egotistical and unprofessional these people were.

"The fact that their former Head of CID had recorded umpteen times, her home address with her force, and that she had frequently been turned out from that address whenever a major incident had taken place, you would think was sufficient," I suggested.

"Absolutely, where do they get these people from?" He was reiterating one of my own favourite sayings when describing the Special Projects Team.

"In addition to that, she had been driven from that same home address to and from work during the time she had been unable to walk unaided, following surgical operations on both feet."

"It makes a nonsense of the need for any surveillance being conducted for those reasons," he remarked.

"And tell me this Bill, what if she had other male friends apart from this pensioner, Arthur Grainger; so, what? What exactly did that prove or have anything to do with the allegations made against her?"

"I have no idea. It does seem as if she is being set up, but why? Can I borrow this for just a couple of days?"

"Show it to your board of directors, Bill, and prove to them the kind of people who have made the complaint against you. Everything contained in that signed authorisation is fiction, which is more likely to have been concocted as an unjustifiable excuse just to put more pressure on an already besieged, Jean Goodman."

The next time we met, was a few days later, when Bill returned the confidential documents to me, explaining that his Board of Directors had accepted that the complaints made against him had been totally unfounded. According to my journalist colleague, his people had referred to the police as being 'bad people, who should behave in a different manner'. The naivety of those who had been responsible for attempting to throw mud at, Jean Goodman through the media, had resulted in the force being justifiably branded as liars, and any credibility they might have had, in particular with the BBC, had now been lost.

"They were fuming and have given me the go ahead for a series of nightly news items outlining the inefficient manner in which your girl has been investigated," he said.

Well, I did say the media was my home territory, and those who thought they were being smart, had encroached on it, only to have lost the support of both newspapers and television. Their scheme aimed towards taking away public support from, Jean Goodman, was about to explode in their faces.

What followed my meetings with, Bill Graveney was the television broadcasts of news items on each night of that week, virtually condemning the police for the role they were playing in the, Jean Goodman Inquiry and sparking a number of enquiries being made from other sources. Questions were asked in the House of Commons relevant to the cost of the Inquiry, which was looking into an allegation of an old man bestowing gifts on a female senior police officer. Criticism of the force came from all directions and I imagined a few individuals at Police Headquarters, squirming behind their desks.

For the first time since the beginning of this bizarre sequence of events, all of my team rejoiced. There was a general feeling that the tide was at last turning in our favour. Personally, I wasn't so optimistic or celebratory. The Special Projects Team was still running the show, and all we had accomplished was to get their backs up. From now on they would be more determined to destroy Jean and those who were siding her. I knew only too well that we would all have to remain on our toes and focus far more than ever before, on what we were getting up to. I told the rest of our team members my feelings and they all agreed, being the true professionals that they were.

As far as our strategy was concerned, I had always insisted with Jean that everything we did should remain transparent, without exaggeration or flowering anything up. I didn't have to tell her that really, but it made me feel good. Everything we recovered or came across would have to be collaborated. All evidential material that supported her claim of innocence, would have to be checked and rechecked. I felt at that stage it would be pointless sending any new material to the police because we had already done that, only to be ignored.

There had been a constant stream of recovered evidential material being sent to Bristol for the attention of, John Mitchell, Jean's solicitor, and I was aware a barrister had been appointed to represent her at trial. In fact, arrangements were being made through Malcolm Richards, for her to travel and meet her new legal representative.

However, I wasn't prepared to turn down the heat, now we had some momentum going, as far as the press was concerned. Following that particular incident, I decided it was time for the, Jean Goodman camp to start throwing a few bombs back in the direction of her accusers. After all, why should she remain silent when she had nothing to hide? Why should she hold her own counsel when people were conniving towards publicly shaming her and doing their best to make her position as a serving police officer, untenable? It was time to kick arse, in my book, and I began to collect a dossier on the media coverage of the case up to that point. Now the bit was between my teeth, I was not prepared to hold back. After all, it was the police who had initially run to the newspapers to reveal, Jean's suspension. They had chosen the battle ground, and we would use it to best advantage.

Chapter Twelve

A meeting of the full team took place in our usual safe location, the small city centre bar, which was free from prying eyes, and I wasted little time in updating everyone on the progress we had made thus far. Both, Neil Rowbotham and, Paul Lownie produced a list of cases in which, Jean Goodman had been involved with investigating over the previous two years. There was no doubting, from the size of the list, she had been an extremely busy lady.

The majority of the cases had been dealt with successfully, but there was one, the lads indicated, which might be of particular interest. It was the very last case she had been involved in, and according to the documentation, had remained undetected.

A young prostitute had been found strangled to death in a high rise flat. There had been no sign of any struggle and initial enquiries made with neighbouring tenants had revealed nothing. It was suspected that the lass had been killed by a client, who it was thought, might well have become over-zealous.

Initially, I had no reason to connect the murder with the events surrounding, Jean, but found myself being drawn towards it, if only because the killer had not been caught. It was one of those types of murders that had always attracted my attention like a magnet. Thinking back, I also believed that it held my interest because, from the brief circumstances surrounding the case, I was of the opinion that it should have been cleared. Now that, Jean Goodman was no longer in charge of the investigation, there was every possibility it would remain undetected, and an opportunity to clear a murder had been missed.

The victim's name was Julie Roberts, and the block of flats in which she'd been killed was situated in the centre of the red-light district, not far from where I met up with, Patch Humpage. Even if the case had nothing to do with what we were enquiring about, I thought by taking a look at it would do no harm. I was well aware that such intention was contradictory to what I had declared before, about not being led astray by red herrings, but there was something about the circumstances of this particular murder that seemed to go beyond that. Call it a sixth sense, but I just couldn't walk away from it.

"Have you found any case in which, Jean Goodman attended with another senior officer?" I asked.

Neil Rowbotham shook his head and explained, "The only senior detective who accompanied her to most of these was her deputy, Mark Grossman. Most of the initial enquiries had been made by the local CID."

I knew that what I had asked for was a long shot but couldn't help but concede, the answer we were all seeking, was lying somewhere in that administrative forest. It was my belief that there existed a nugget of gold hidden within the depths of some investigation or Inquiry involving, Jean, which once uncovered would provide us with all the answers.

I was under no disillusionment though. Apart from being a Senior Investigating Officer, the lady had other strings to her bow. Of course, she was a Hostage Negotiator, in addition to, and on occasions, being asked to investigate internal serious allegations. During her time in office, Jean had spread her wings beyond the force boundary, and had been engaged in re-structuring Regional Crime Squads, and measuring the cost efficiency of Forensic Laboratories. And yet, I favoured the more operational side of her job, and asked my people to dig deeper. But there was one other subject we had not yet approached.

I turned to, Sandra Jenson and Rolly Guthridge and asked them to look further into Chief Superintendent Jean Goodman's personal background.

"I need to know as much as we can find out about former boyfriends, particularly any who might have been serving officers."

They both looked at me sheepishly and I explained further, "I know you will be prying into something which should remain private, but at the moment, everything is on the table, and I want you to act as covertly as possible."

"Can't we just ask her?" Sandra suggested.

"No, because there might be someone she is too embarrassed to mention, and that would be the kind of man I am looking for."

"A married man you mean."

"Possibly." I continued, addressing the same couple. "Try and find out if there have been any threatening remarks made about, Jean Goodman, by members of the Surveillance Unit, especially individuals involved in that scandal you uncovered." That was more to their liking, but I still needed that sweep of Jean's past to be completed as a matter of urgency.

During the time we were trying so hard to find a motive that went beyond what people would generally believe, was all to do with the allegations made against Jean, her solicitor, John Mitchell had also been probing into his client's case, believing she was innocent of any wrong doing. John was a young, tall man with dark hair cut short, and the kind of fresh face, which told you all you wanted to know. He was an honest lawyer, who cared for people.

Having seen the way in which his client had been handled during that initial interview at Police Headquarters, which had followed her arrest, he had been appalled by her treatment and remained in a state of consternation and anger. He also resented the arrogant way in which the interviewing officers had ignored certain legal requirements and was still patiently waiting for her persecutors to fulfil their legal obligations, by disclosing what evidence they were supposed to have in their possession. In fact, he was at that time, putting together an application to the High Court for a writ to be issued for that same disclosure.

Not having had any initial intention of travelling with, Malcolm Richards and Jean, down to the Inns of Court in London, where they were to meet for the first time, the Queens Counsel who would be representing the interests of the defence at the forthcoming trial, John Mitchell had insisted I attended. So, I did so, but it wasn't for me to sit in the meeting between Jean and her counsel; that was a part of Malcolm's terms of reference.

Whilst they were discussing the case in one room, her solicitor escorted me into another, where we sat at a large oval shaped table, and I patiently waited to find out what exactly he required from me.

"One of the major issues I have been fencing with all of this time, is how on earth, Arthur Grainger, could have been manipulated to make a complaint against my client," he explained.

"Perhaps he hasn't made a complaint?"

"Then she would have no case to answer. Mr. Grainger has to be the main witness for the prosecution."

"I can only assume his daughter has been pulling the strings then. There is no one else we are aware of."

The solicitor then took a type written statement from some other papers lodged inside a briefcase and passed it across the table for me to read. It had been made by, Arthur Grainger and contained his signature on every page.

"The police have sent this to me, I suppose to try and appease me as a result of constantly demanding disclosure and threatening to go before a High Court Judge for a writ to force them into undertaking their legal obligations. It was sent by Superintendent Snipe."

"With no other documents?"

"No, but I shall persist in demanding full disclosure from them, but you might find the second page of the elderly man's statement makes interesting reading."

He remained quiet, allowing me to scan over the document and I quickly recognised the paragraphs which he was referring to on the second page. The eighty-six-year-old statement maker alleged that, Jean Goodman had given him lifts to church in her car on numerous occasions. On a number of those, she would stop to kiss him. Not a friendly kiss, the statement described, but a full blown, tongue down your throat kiss, which according to the old man, had left him in a dizzy each time he had been a recipient of such devotion.

The statement also went on to confirm that at no time, did the lady ever try to solicit gifts from him, and everything he had purchased for her, was of his own making, which at least took some of the sting out of the fraudulent elements of the allegations. However, the fact that she had acted so improperly would suffice to show that she was deliberately coercing the pensioner into treating her favourably.

"Now, let me ask you this," her solicitor said, after I had finished reading the document, "Does that sound like reasonable behaviour by my client, when in the company of an eighty-six-year-old gentleman?"

"No, never. That is totally contradictory to the kind of woman I know, Jean Goodman to be."

John Mitchell smiled, before producing yet another statement, which he held on to. He then explained, "Professor Henry Waddington is an old friend of mine who works at the University of Toronto in Canada. Henry is also a psychiatrist who is a widely recognised expert in a condition, which he believes, Arthur Grainger is suffering from."

I thought for a minute the lawyer was going to suggest that, Grainger was some kind of pervert, which would have been beyond even my vivid imagination, but he didn't.

"My friend is currently in the UK visiting family, and I had an opportunity over dinner one night, to discuss the case with him. According to, Henry, the condition is recognised when an individual genuinely believes that another person is in love with them," John continued, "A delusional disorder with paranoid tendencies, known as Eratomania."

"And you suspect the old man could have been suffering from this condition?"

"The keyword is delusional. You see, according to Henry Waddington, a person suffering from such a condition, honestly believes that he has an admirer who is infatuated by them, so much so, they imagine incidents which they believe to be true, albeit they never happened."

"It would certainly explain how the police came to believe everything the old man told them."

"It usually occurs apparently in older gentlemen or ladies, but I've made a request for the prosecution to confirm whether or not their main witness has been psychiatrically examined, which I suspect has not been the case. If that is so, then we can submit a request to the court that the witness is unreliable as a result of him suffering from Eratomania."

I was intrigued by this particular solicitor's dedication and commitment to his client and enquired whether he thought we should ask for the old man to be examined ourselves.

"Ah, that might be difficult," he said, "And I very much doubt the prosecution would agree to that. However, by the time we get to trial, Henry Waddington will be back in Canada, but he has offered to return and give evidence about the subject of Eratomania, if required. He is convinced from the circumstances I related to him, that his specialist subject is present here, and is quite willing to swear an oath by it."

Such a medical opinion would undoubtedly strengthen the case for the defence, adding another string to our bow. I congratulated the lawyer on the way in which he was handling the defence for Jean and then asked him a pertinent question.

"What do you honestly think her chances are, of being acquitted I mean?"

Guardedly he answered, "Extremely high, from the evidence you have gathered and forwarded to me. All we can do is try and cover every angle of the prosecution's case and then wait for the jury to decide."

"How can we do that when they have failed to disclose what evidence they have?"

"Exactly; but believe me when I tell you that such deficiency can only work against them. I am really surprised and slightly confused by their behaviour."

That was fair comment, and I later returned from London with Jean and Malcom Richards, explaining what, John Mitchell had told me.

Jean was enthusiastic about the news, but Malcolm, being similar to myself, remained a little sceptical. We both strongly believed now, that there was a reason for what had happened; a reason which we had not yet identified. Although remaining confident we would eventually reveal the true motive, my problem was, that when we finally did so, we would most likely uncover something which was extremely serious in its nature, and frighteningly damaging to the individual behind the motive. Strangely, my thoughts returned to the murder of the young prostitute and I wondered how her parents must have been feeling. That was if the poor lass had any. I needed to find out more.

Chapter Thirteen

At one end of the spacious office on the top floor of Police Headquarters, stood a large desk, beneath a portrait of the Queen hanging from the far wall. Down the one side of the room were a number of picture windows through which various skyscrapers could be viewed, protruding up from the city centre, above the roofs of small buildings. A large highly polished rectangular Mahogany table was positioned at the opposite end of the room to where the desk was located and surrounded by twelve chairs. The Deputy Chief Constable, Adrian Plum and Superintendent Robert Snipe occupied two of them, one egotistical individual, constantly aware of his second highest rank in the force, and the other, widely known for his garrulous manner. Each senior officer had a large file of papers laid out before him and appeared to be in a relatively sombre mood. This was the inner sanctum, where individuals attended only by invitation, and the two visitors had been summoned to attend.

The Chief Constable, Christopher Hartley, sat at one end of the table, looking inquisitively at his two officers, who had already been informed as to the purpose of their calling. They were there to update their leader on the progress of the ongoing Inquiry into Chief Superintendent Goodman. He was a tall, thin man with dark hair, greying at the sides and with constantly alert and probing eyes, which tended to look through people, rather than just at them.

"So, Adrian, where exactly are we with this?" the senior man enquired, "As I understand we are now entering the third month since Miss Goodman's suspension was initiated."

"Our enquiries are ongoing Chief Constable, and I understand there is still a lot of investigative work to be done on the previous activities of the woman."

The highest-ranking officer in the force appeared to sigh, as he sat back, away from the table, grasping both hands on his lap.

"Tell me then, what is the exact nature of these activities we suspect our former Head of CID of having been involved in?"

The DCC looked across at, Robert Snipe, who took his cue and began to detail a number of suspected corrupt practices he and his team believed, Jean Goodman had been connected with.

"We have received a number of allegations made against Miss Goodman, sir, suggesting that she has been cavorting with undesirable members of the criminal fraternity, including international drugs dealers, and individuals connected to the unlawful practice of influencing juries... I believe that..."

"These are extremely serious allegations, Superintendent," the Chief Constable said, interrupting, Snipe's flow, with a derisory smile on his face, "What are the sources of your information?"

Snipe moved uncomfortably in his seat, and answered slightly nervously, "Well, the majority have come from the anonymous Red Line." He was referring to a facility where members of the force could report instances of corruption without being identified.

"Have you any absolute evidence to show that, Jean Goodman committed these atrocities?" Christopher Hartley asked, looking directly at Adrian Plum, "Or has in any way been associated with such serious allegations?"

"Hopefully, we will. That's why we need to continue with our investigations."

"So, all we have at present, are a number of suggestions coming from a pool of anonymous subscribers, who could be any of a number of officers who have cause to resent the former Head of CID, in particular, individuals who she has been responsible for transferring out of her department because of ineptitude or other possibly more serious behaviour."

There was a short period of silence, as both Plum and Snipe looked at each other for inspiration. Then the DCC hastily referred to the circumstances, which led to, Jean Goodman's suspension in the first instance.

"I have no doubt, she deliberately solicited benefits from an eighty-year old pensioner, who remains today, a clearly thinking man, who is coherent and not lacking in honesty."

"Yes, yes, I am aware of that and await the outcome of the trial with interest, but it does appear gentlemen that our lady has a great deal of support from the media, including a number of Members of Parliament who have written to me, requesting details of the cost of the Inquiry thus far. How much is the overall cost at present?"

"That is difficult to estimate at present Chief Constable," Snipe replied, "Because of the various investigative elements that have been involved."

"You mean Superintendent, elements such as those preventing Miss Goodman from visiting her parents' graves or preventing her from worshipping at her local church."

"There are witnesses who …"

"Enough," the Chief Constable demanded, once again cutting off the lower ranking man, "I can inform you gentlemen that the overall cost of your Inquiry to date exceeds one million pounds." He paused to observe the reaction of the other two.

Adrian Plum looked genuinely surprised at the figure, but his Superintendent just sat there, looking indifferently and unmoved.

Christopher Hartley then turned to his deputy and advised, with some authority in his voice, that the man lifted the ban on the suspended officer attending her church and visiting her parents graves forthwith.

"We must appear gentlemen," he continued, "To be fair and just, with all of our internal investigations. In reality we must also, I suggest, continue our enquiries with the utmost objectivity, which I might add, does not appear to be have been the case thus far, according to what I have observed and been told."

Plum appeared to be about to make his own opinion known, but was abruptly stopped by a raised palm, before the Chief Constable continued, "The longer this Inquiry goes on, the more likelihood there will be of us being exposed to further severe criticism and ridicule. I do not think it wise to prolong your investigations further and suggest, Adrian, you rein your dogs in, and concentrate on the allegations for which Miss Goodman is to stand trial. Nothing more will be gained by delving into other matters which in all probability, do not exist and for which, we could be accused of conducting nothing more than a witch hunt against the woman."

They both disagreed with the Chief Constable's conclusions but neither intended putting up any argument. Above all, they were two extremely ambitious men who were looking to their futures and to argue or confront a Chief Constable's way of thinking could be disastrous.

Malcolm Richards arrived at, Jean Goodman's house in a fluster. He resembled the owner of a Derby winner and couldn't wait to share the good news with her. He had considered phoning but wanted to see the look of joy on her face when he told her that a decision had been made to lift the ban imposed on, Jean, prohibiting the lady from visiting her church and parents' graves.

She was delighted, and immediately burst into tears, before reaching for her coat. There was no time to waste. Those graves had been left unattended for far too long, and she was desperate to place fresh flowers down and generally tidy up around them. She politely rejected an offer from, Malcolm to drive her to the church, intending to purchase bouquets on the way.

As he returned to his vehicle, watching her leave the house, he wondered if the next good news would contain a declaration that the criminal case against, Jean, had been dropped completely. We are all entitled to dream, but his was just a case of wishful thinking.

After I received the same news in a phone call from, Malcolm, of course I was happy for, Jean, but remained sceptical that such a concession by the enemy had not come from any intention to do the lady a favour, but more from the image they were putting up for the benefit of the media. I was truly convinced the power of the press had brought about this welcome result for, Jean, but it was of no consequence. The main thing was, they had finally conceded to lifting, what had always been, a cruel and unnecessary restriction.

In the company of, Andy Greatrix and, Dave Stewart, I visited the same tower block in which the young prostitute, Julie Roberts, had been murdered. It was typical of all the residences left standing within the red-light district. Professional sex workers plied their trade on virtually every street corner, although it was broad daylight, and no lift interior, or wall inside the tower blocks, was free from multi-coloured, sprayed on expletives and various crude caricatures. It all added to an environment of degradation.

We found the flat which had been the scene of the murder to be void, with the door secured with a padlock and chain, preventing any forced entry.

There were three other flats on the same floor, and we knocked on the doors of each of them, but without receiving any response, except the one situated opposite the victim's. An elderly lady, who gave her name as being Mrs. Thomas, answered the door. She was a pleasant lady who described to us how various numbers of strange men frequently visited, Julie Roberts flat during the day and night.

I asked if she remembered any one of them in particular, but she couldn't.

"Did you ever have occasion to speak with Miss Roberts?" I asked.

She shook her head but did confess to very occasionally exchanging a greeting with the young woman. Then, as if she suddenly remembered one individual visitor she explained, "He was a rat faced little man with his hair made up of strings."

"A Rastafarian gentleman," I suggested.

"I think so," the old lady agreed, not really knowing what a Rastafarian was, "He was always visiting. Most days I would see him come out of the lift and bang on the door. She always let him inside."

"How long did he stay, have you any idea?" Dave Stewart asked.

"No, but he did visit more than once on some days."

"How had he used to dress?"

"When I saw him, he was always wearing the same clothes, a T shirt and pair of grubby jeans. I forgot to mention him to the other officers who I spoke to at the time. Could you tell them for me?"

"Of course," I said, knowing she was referring to those who would have been engaged in the initial stages of the investigation, "But is there anything else you can tell us about this individual. He was a Rastafarian, you say. What was his skin like, dark, light..?"

"He had light skin with one of those short. pointed beards on his chin."

"A Rastafarian with a goatee beard." I was quietly convinced that the lady was probably describing the murdered girl's pimp, who should by rights, have been the prime suspect. It could be, of course, the man would already have been interviewed and we had to bear that in mind.

A few more questions revealed nothing more, and we left the neighbour after thanking her for her assistance.

Unfortunately, the description we had been given of the frequent caller, would have fitted a host of visitors to the area. We needed to know more if we were to identify our mystery man and I knew exactly where that information might be stored.

After leaving my two colleagues, it was time to pay another visit to, Patch Humpage. If there was any living being in this metropolis who would know the frequent visitor to Julie Roberts place of business, it was the man from the gutters.

Chapter Fourteen

The man in the white mackintosh, wearing a broad rimmed trilby hat, stepped into the hotel reception and ignoring the booking-in desk, made his way past the cluster of decorative tables and soft chairs, until reaching the cocktail bar. As he removed his hat and coat, quickly scanning his eyes over what few late afternoon drinkers were present, he instantly recognised the gentleman he had come to meet, sitting alone, near to some large French windows which looked out on to picturesque and cultivated tiered gardens.

He made his approach and the small, rounded man with a cheerful smile and bald head, stood to welcome him with an extended hand. His appearance was that of a business man, wearing a dark suit with a waistcoat displaying a gold watch chain across is mid-rift. As he ordered drinks, his visitor carefully placed his hat and outer garment on a nearby chair, before taking a seat opposite. Both men then waited for the waiter to bring two glasses of Pimm's and Tonic, with the newcomer showing slight signs of discomfiture and quickly glancing around the room to ensure no one was within earshot. From that moment, they both spoke quietly and with purpose, careful not to mention names or any other information that might assist in identifying the pair.

"I received your initial instructions," the bald-headed man confirmed, "And my contact has agreed to fulfil the agreement. However, he has raised a small problem."

"And what small problem would that be? He wants more money, am I right?"

"That's not the real difficulty which confronts him. He believes the fact that the target is a serving police officer, adds a far greater element of risk to the enterprise he is willing to undertake. Also, a female being involved, serves to add further aggravation to the circumstances of his task, which he feels justifies him in demanding a higher commission. I'm sure you can appreciate his concerns."

"How much higher?"

"Five thousand in addition to the originally agreed price."

The customer raised his eyes and hesitated.

"My contact is the best in the business and has completed successful assignments all over Europe. You are guaranteed a successful result without any risk to yourself," the bald-headed man explained, "It's a matter of whether you feel the price is worth it or not."

"Thirty thousand in total is a lot of money?"

The supplier nodded and added, "A successful conclusion in a high-risk business is costly, if you want the best there is. Of course, my own commission is included in that sum."

"Very well, when will your contact complete the job?"

"From the information you have provided, I suspect completion will be sooner rather than later, but I can assure you, my man will not rush things. He will need a short period of surveillance and research before striking, but you will be notified by one singular phone call, once the agreement has been concluded."

"No, a phone call will not be necessary. I will find out soon enough. But tell me, what kind of man is your contact?"

The bald-headed man smiled, and took a gulp of his Pimms, before announcing, "That is not within my terms of reference. We are professionals and the least you know of personal details, the more beneficial it is to yourself. However, there is just one further stipulation, which is not negotiable. My contact will require full payment in cash, obviously, before undertaking the project."

The visitor finished his drink and stood, taking hold of his hat and coat, before nodding at his cheerful looking business associate and declaring, "The money will be available the day after tomorrow."

"Then I shall await your pleasure here, shall we say the same time?"

Again, the man nodded, before turning and leaving. Would the product he had just purchased be worth the expenditure involved? In his view no, but at least he would have removed the danger to himself.

I found Patch Humpage sitting on his usual bar stool inside his preferred safe haven and couldn't help but notice a number of grazes on both sides of his face. One eye was beginning to swell up and it was obvious he'd taken a beating, which wasn't the first time the undercover cop had been involved in some kind of physical skirmish.

"What does the other bloke look like, Patch?" I quietly asked.

"I've no idea, he caught me in a dark alley, when I was half pissed, but I'll tell you this, he limped away after I managed to stick a blade in his leg."

How could any reasonably thinking human being live this kind of life, I asked myself, but thank God, this lad did. He was more valuable to me, than any paid and professional informant could have been. I immediately bought a couple of pints of ale, served in those grimy glasses.

"How is my favourite lady dick bearing up?" he asked, wincing slightly as he tried to smile.

"Better than the last time I saw you, but I wanted to mention another job to you."

"You have my undivided attention but do allow for the occasional facial tweak or two, when my ribs remind me of the pummelling they've just been subjected to."

"Do you recall a few months ago, a prostitute by the name of, Julie Roberts being topped over in Grimshaw House?" I was referring to the name of the tower block in which the victim lived.

Patch answered without hesitation. "She was one of Laser Johnson's girls, a young West Indian who runs a string of them around the district. Mouthy little bastard who carries a chiv up his arse and is an established figure in vice and drugs."

"Small, thinly built geezer with dreadlocks in a T shirt and jeans?"

"That's him, flies around like some kind of sunbeam, here one day, gone the next. He knocks around in an old red Cortina or did so, the last time I set eyes on him, giving one of his girls a good hiding in Victoria Street in the middle of the night."

"Sounds like the kind of bloke you wouldn't want your daughter to bring home. Could he have strangled his girl to death?"

Patch didn't bother giving the question any consideration, confessing convincingly, "Who knows? He's got a temper, okay. But only where women are concerned. Put a bloke up against him and he'd shit himself. Having said that, it wouldn't stop the little bastard from sticking you in the back as you walked away."

I closed my eyes as I took a gulp of the potion that was resting on the top of the bar, and asked, "Where do I find him, Patch?"

"With difficulty. He's a fly by night, who can turn up anywhere at any time. The best way to feel his collar is to sit on one of his girl's and wait for him to turn up."

He could see I'd hit a hard place and quickly suggested I sat on a girl by the name of, Roberta Cummings, who frequented a local nightclub known as, The Red Parrot.

"Bobby Cummings is Laser Johnson's favourite girl, only because she's never short of custom and brings in a lot of dough for him. She's also an intelligent girl, who would have known, Julie Roberts. She works to get enough money to keep a young daughter in a private school, so it might be wise to have a word with her, before going for her pimp. If you put up enough readies on the table, she'd sell out her own mother, as would any of our ladies of the night."

"Do you know mate, I think I might just do that."

"Remember though, you ain't a cop any longer, but these people will still smell you out, as soon as you break into their air space."

"I remember only too well, Patch."

Whether it was the way we were dressed, or just the official looks on our faces, there was no one to challenge us as we entered through the narrow doorway of The Red Parrot Night Club. Or it might have been because the same establishment was such a seedy looking dominion of debauchery, rarely visited by the cops, we were just ignored. Climbing up a narrow, dark staircase, with a much fitter, Dave Stewart following closely behind, we eventually reached the main bar room. Not surprisingly, it was packed out with representatives from most walks of life. There were alcoholics, former bankers who had fallen on harder times, pimps, prostitutes, milkmen, dustmen and gents who were there merely to drink the night away, whilst trying to deal with their sorrows.

The cost of the drinks was an insult to normal, reasonable people, so was the price I had to pay the barman, just for him to point out the girl we had come to see, who was sitting in one darkened corner with an obvious potential client. From a distance, Roberta Cummings was not unattractive, and was displaying the kind of hard set smile, which was developed from a vast amount of experience in having to appear pleasant to all kinds of male punters. The girl's profession attracted quite a variety, from the very cruel to the most naïve, but I had no doubt, as was the case with most punters seeking the company of a lady of the night, she would be quite capable of dealing with whatever was thrown in her direction.

The man she was pawing all over, and who was obviously paying for her drinks, looked like some Irish stevedore; huge in build with biceps protruding beneath a blue patterned shirt. If it hadn't been for our own prowess at removing such obstacles, it would have taken a crane to have lifted him out of there.

I nodded at, Dave and within a few seconds, he'd spoken a few words in the man's ear, before standing back and watching him leave hastily, with a look of daggers in the girl's eyes. She was still fuming and voicing her opinion on Dave's character and birth right, when I sat next to her.

"Sorry about that, Bobby," I said apologetically, "But we wish to make you an offer."

Her demeanour immediately changed and her eyes brightened when she saw me pull out a fifty-pound note.

"Well, I don't usually do twosomes," she said, stretching to make her bosom more appealing, "But for that much bread, I'm sure I can make an exception."

"There's no need to luv," I quietly answered, "It's information we're after and you don't have to shift your arse off that seat, for the price of a night's work."

She stared at me in silence momentarily, before asking in a lowered voice, "What kind of information?" One hand reached for the note I was holding, but I managed to snatch it away, demanding the information came first.

"I understand you knew Julie Roberts, the girl who was done in not so long back?"

"So that's it," she said, "A pair of dicks."

"No, just interested parties, trying to put our hands on her killer."

"Well, I know nothing mister. It's got nothing to do with me."

"What about Laser Johnson? Would he know anything about it?"

Quickly, she looked around her, just to see if her pimp was nearby, but he wasn't. We had already checked.

"Do you think he could have strangled her to death?"

She shook her head, and I wasn't sure whether that denial came from fear or honest assumption.

"I hear he's good at beating up his girls from time to time," I suggested.

"Then you've heard wrong mister. He ain't the bloke you're looking for."

She grinned nervously, obviously focusing on how she could get her hands on that fifty quid that was still grasped tightly in my hand.

"Then have you got any idea who is?"

Again, she shook her head.

"Take your pick darling, from any of the weirdos who visited Julie."

"I can't, they're all capable of doing that, when it comes to paying up front."

"Then earn this fifty-quid and give us a few prime candidates."

"Look," she said, placing a hand around a half empty glass of Pernod, "There's them who like to be violent and them that likes you to be violent. There's them who likes to be tied up and spanked, and them that prefers just to be tied up and cry their eyes out. Shall I go on?"

"We're looking for somebody who stood out from the rest of the clientele, Bobby, some individual who might be a bit different from the rest. A man for example, who might be loaded with money, or was perhaps the kind of pervert who went too far."

Again, she shook her head, but was much calmer this time, obviously trying to recall someone who might have fitted the bill. At least the girl was trying, but then had to concede, "No, I don't know of anybody like that who worked with Julie."

"Where can I find Laser then?" I asked, believing everything the girl had said up to then.

She lowered her voice, and with a look of mischief, surprisingly confirmed, "He's at the bar, looking across at your back mister."

I quickly glanced across at, Dave Stewart, who nodded his understanding of what was to happen next.

"This fifty-pound note is yours to keep, Bobby," I told the girl, "But I need you to step outside into the street with me."

"Why, where we going?"

"Nowhere, just to the street outside, and then you can come back here if you want."

She nodded. I stood up, and she took hold of my arm with that plastic grin back across her face, before we both made our exit.

We slowly made our way down the stairs; a lady of the night escorting her latest client, back to her safe haven. After reaching the street outside, I handed the money to her, before quickly heading back inside the club. Before reaching the top of the stairs, Laser Johnson was coming down them, heading straight for me with an arm pinioned up his back, and Dave Stewart breathing down the pimp's neck. We both hustled him out of the club, into the back of my car, which was parked out front. Once we had him secured on the back seat, I took a six-inch blade I found strapped to the lower part of his leg, before leaving him with Dave, whilst I jumped into the driver's seat and drove away.

We didn't have to go far, before I found a patch of wasteland, where it was as black as pitch. The unofficial interrogation of the murder suspect was about to begin in earnest and this feller in particular was really and truly looking forward to what was about to follow

Chapter Fifteen

During the time I spent as a serving detective, I had always regarded those who managed the activities of prostitutes, repulsive. In my view they were the lowest of the low, living off the earnings of others, at the same time securing their positions by bullying and fear. The girls who worked for them, suffered greatly at the hands of their pimps, finally having to perform their antics for whatever crumbs their guardians decided to pay them. So, I found no great displeasure in smacking this particular miscreant in the mouth a couple of times, just to persuade him it was in his interests to remain civil towards us.

Of course, the man denied any knowledge of the murder of one of his girls. We had been anticipating that, and constantly swore and blasphemed, in between trying to put on a convincing display of innocence.

"But it was your job to protect her, shithole," I explained, "That's why she would have handed her money across to you."

"Listen man, why would I bump off one of my girls," he pleaded, "I ain't admitting nothing, but ask yourself this question filth, why would I snap the neck of a good source of income."

It was obvious, Laser Johnson believed we were cops, and I couldn't think of any reason to try and dissuade him of that falsity.

"You my son, are going away for a long time for that girl's murder."

"Why me man? Why pick on me? I ain't done nothing, I keep telling you."

"You had an argument with your girl, which went further than you expected and, during that confrontation, you wrapped your hands around her throat and choked her to death."

He slumped back and made a hissing sound between his teeth.

Dave planted a punch in the man's mid-rift, causing him to sit up straight again, and explained that every time he decided to sit back like that, he would get the same treatment. After coughing and spluttering, he continued to plead his innocence, until it became boring.

"Well my diminutive little friend," I said in a cold voice, "Either you are coming with us for the big jump, or you can return to that rat hole we've taken you from, if you finger the geezer who did choke the life out of your girl."

"If I knew that, don't you think I'd be chewing his balls," Laser snapped back, with meaningful intent in his wide eyes. There was most definitely a hint of truth in his voice, and I was beginning to be persuaded.

"You must have known her clients, so which one was the most likely to lose it in such a fatal way?"

He shook his head, and looked down at his pants, suddenly realising he pissed himself. I didn't think we'd gone that far with him. Mind you, Dave Stewart wasn't exactly the innocent looking type, and resembled more of a serial killer than a serial killer would have done.

"Tell me this then, Laser, amongst Julie's clients, was any of them filth?"

He looked astonished at the question, as if suspecting we were after putting away one of our own.

Then he surprised us both by admitting, "There was one, but I never met him. Julie mentioned she was seeing to some copper, but that was all, I swear."

A dozen or so more questions followed, such as, what did he look like, did she give any name, rank and similar queries, but nothing more could be dragged out of the pimp. Finally, we both realised we had just about extracted every last piece of useful information from our man, so dumped him back outside the front of The Red Parrot. We left him still swearing and spitting.

The night's exercise hadn't been completely futile. Okay, so it was like pulling teeth, but I felt we were slowly getting somewhere. If what, Johnson had told us was the truth, a police officer had been one of Julie Robert's customers, that was certainly something to bear in mind in the future, but now I had to divert my mind back to the case in hand and leave the detective work to the professionals.

The day that, Jean Goodman was to make her initial appearance before the court finally arrived. Although it was to be a preliminary hearing before a Stipendiary Magistrate, to examine the evidence against her, she was obviously suffering intensely. Her outward appearance remained calm and dignified, but I knew that beneath that surface, there was an ongoing war between conflicting emotions. The reason for the lady's inner strife was due to the embarrassment she was about to experience at the hands of the legal profession, having given evidence in the same Magistrates Court on numerous occasions throughout her police career. Now she would have to stand in the dock, as the prisoner, accused of fraud and knowing that everyone inside that courtroom would have already decided she was guilty. There was no doubt that, once having examined whatever evidence they were going to bring against, Jean Goodman, the Stipendiary Magistrate would inevitably commit her to take her trial at the Crown Court.

When she surrendered to the prison officers who were in the dock, both myself and, Malcolm Richards were standing beside her. Earlier, I had told her what to expect and to remember throughout the proceedings which were to follow, that no matter what was said, she would be going home, later that day. She needed above all else, to retain her dignity and not show the reprobates who had put her there, that she was in fear of them.

When the prison officer to whom she reported opened the door to the dock, he explained she would have to go down below, and wait in one of the cells for her name to be called.

I could see the colour drain from Jean's face, and explained to the officer who she was, begging that she be allowed to remain seated at the back of the court until her time came.

"And you are sir?" the robust man with the flushed round face enquired.

But before I could answer, Malcolm Richards declared openly, "I am Chief Superintendent Richards and can guarantee this lady will remain at the back of the court, sitting on those benches, until you call her into the dock."

The prison officer was obviously reluctant to break with tradition, but eventually succumbed and agreed to our request, provided that Jean never left the confines of the court room. So, the wait began with our charge sitting on the hard-wooden bench between the two of us. A wait which was to test my patience, but obviously tested our girl's resolve and temperament even further.

John Mitchell soon appeared, together with a young female clerk, and immediately sat down to explain to his client what was to take place that morning. The solicitor appeared very confident and virtually swore that she would be granted bail, following the formal committal proceedings. He was obviously playing his role out with the intention of keeping Jean calm and optimistic, but personally I believed he'd failed. She was her own person and no stranger to court proceedings. She also knew exactly what the likely outcome of the Hearing would be. It was just the thought of the embarrassment of having to stand alone in that bloody dock, that was rattling her cage.

Then, Robert Snipe and a couple of his cronies made an appearance, sitting down on a row of benches behind the witness box which were there just for the use of police officers and members of the press. I couldn't resist a thought which came to me there and then, so, using my own press pass, stepped past the usher and took up a seat immediately behind the Superintendent.

Leaning forward, I whispered in the clown's ear, "You do know she's innocent."

"Is she," he replied, half turning his head to see who the cheeky bastard was who had the audacity to speak with him.

"We're almost there," I continued to say, "To prove her innocence I mean, but more importantly, we have enough to put a few of you monkeys in the dock over there, to face charges of conspiring to interfere with the course of justice and commit perjury on signed statements containing the formal caution."

I then stood, having said my peace, and returned to Jean and Malcolm. Okay, so my words might not have carried much weight with Snipe, but by sharing them with him, made me feel a lot better.

The Stipendiary Magistrate entered the courtroom and everyone stood to their feet. He was an elderly gentleman with a round pale and puckered face, above three chins. He was wearing a high winged collar and black tie and had a small pair of spectacles perched on the end of a flat nose. There was a definite similarity between the official and some of the characters found in novels written by Charles Dickens, and I wondered whether he would stay awake to see out the conclusion of the proceedings.

He mumbled something incoherently to his clerk who was seated just in front and below him, and the same prison officer who we had spoken with earlier, opened the gate to the dock and called out, Jean Goodman's name, staring straight at her.

I could feel, Jean trembling as she stood and stepped across, before walking into the dock to face the Stipendiary.

The clerk read out her name and she answered quietly, confirming they had got it right.

Then the committal proceedings got under way, with Snipe taking an oath in the witness box and introducing a number of exhibits, mostly documentary, but did include the items of cheap jewellery recovered from the accused's house. Throughout his evidence, Jean was allowed to sit down, and when the Superintendent in charge of the case had finished producing the exhibits, which would be produced once again at the lady's trial, he left the witness box. Everyone then had to wait in silence, whilst the same Examining Justice signed various authorities and recognitions.

Finally, he looked up and asked the prisoner to stand, which Jean did so. He then mumbled the fact that she would be committed to take her trial at the Crown Court and asked her solicitor if he wished to apply for bail.

John Mitchell stood to his feet and applied on, Jean's behalf.

The Stipendiary then turned to the prosecution solicitor and asked if there was any objection, and much to our horror, a female lawyer, who, up until then hadn't spoken more than three words, declared that there was a formal objection to bail, before calling Superintendent Snipe back into the witness box.

Jean's head immediately spun round and the pathetic, pleading look in her eyes hit me with the force of a tidal wave.

"Whatever are the bastards up to now, Malc?" I asked Malcolm Richards, in almost a whisper.

He just sat there in disbelief, obviously as stunned as I was.

"Get your act together, you might have to give character evidence on her behalf," I whispered, before quietly making my way through the court room until I was sitting directly behind, Jean's solicitor, John Mitchell, at the same time as our man, Snipe was being sworn in, yet again.

"Chief Superintendent Richards will give character evidence if needed," I whispered in the lawyer's ear, knowing it was only a flimsy offer of support.

"He won't be," he quickly answered back.

"Tell the court officer, on what grounds do you object to the accused being granted bail," the floosy from the Crown Prosecutions Service asked.

Snipe stood with a straight back and open face, addressing the Stipendiary, as the lying bastard outlined his well-rehearsed objections.

According to the officer, there was a likelihood that, if released, the prisoner would interfere with witnesses. Bollocks. Also, if she was granted bail there was every likelihood she would abscond prior to her court date for trial. More bollocks. Finally, she had a history of psychiatric problems and it was suspected she could harm herself. Someone had been talking out of school.

John Mitchell then rose to his feet, having been invited to cross examine the witness.

He was smiling pleasantly, as he first addressed the Superintendent with an opening salvo relevant to the allegation his client would interfere with witnesses, asking what witnesses were there, who could possibly be interfered with by the accused.

Snipe made mention of the Grainger family and further added that they were living in fear of the defendant.

Still smiling, the defence lawyer asked, on what grounds were they living in fear of his client.

Snipe looked sheepishly, when he answered, "They are frightened that she might approach them."

"For what purpose, to drink tea with them, or have lunch perhaps. My client's social circle goes beyond an eighty-six-year-old pensioner and his daughter, sir, and I might add that, why, if that was the case, had she not approached them all the time she has been waiting to appear before this court today?"

The Stipendiary nodded his head and grunted something beneath his breath, which no one in the room could possibly have made out.

John Mitchell then returned his gaze back to the witness in the box, and reminded, Mr. Snipe of the second objection to bail, which was the fear that the defendant might abscond.

"On what grounds exist, pray tell the court, which have assisted you in reaching that opinion?"

Snipe had no real answer, except he thought the defendant was unbalanced in her mind and there was a possibility she would not turn up for her trial. It was a feeble excuse and virtually everyone present in that room, knew that was the case.

"Sir," John Mitchell said, once again addressing the Stipendiary, "My client intends to plead 'Not Guilty' to the charges laid against her, and I might add there is a strong case for the defence. She is a serving Detective Chief Superintendent who, although currently suspended from duty, has no intention of absconding and failing to face up to her responsibilities. Where would she go, if she did? Furthermore, she would be quite willing to surrender her passport if required."

There was another nod of the head and mumbling under the breath from the old man on the bench.

Jean's defence lawyer then addressed the third and final objection put forward by, Robert Snipe.

"You have told the court, whilst on oath officer, that my client has a history of psychiatric problems. From which source did you get that allegation?"

Snipe fumbled with his words, obviously in a dither and not having expected such a robust cross-examination. Finally, he told the court that he couldn't disclose the source because it would not be in the public interest.

I thought that, John Mitchell was about to leap into the witness box and thump him, but the lawyer was a true professional, and with all the calmness and deliberation in his locker, quietly pointed out to the Stipendiary that his client was responsible for a budget of over sixty million pounds and had been responsible for the management of over eight thousand personnel.

"In addition, sir, she has successfully led investigations into more than thirty serious offences of crime, including murder and two attempted terrorist attacks in this city. I believe that is not the conduct of someone suffering from some psychiatric difficulty and submit to you, that in the absence of any medical evidence to the contrary, the suggestion that she would harm herself is total fiction."

"Yes, yes, I hear what you say sir," the old man said, with everyone at least hearing those words from his garbled mouth.

"I must also inform the court, that part of my client's defence will cast assertions on the way in which the investigation into her, has been conducted by the police, and therefore submit that she be granted unconditional bail until she has to surrender herself to the Crown Court."

He sat down, and I waited for the Stipendiary to retire to consider the bail application. But there was no need. The old man didn't flinch a muscle and just ruled that Jean would be granted unconditional bail.

There were tears in her eyes when she left the dock, and both myself and, Malcolm Richards ushered her away, out of the court room, before any of the opposition saw her distressed state. That was the first legal victory we had achieved over them, which made us all far more optimistic. There was no doubt though, in my mind, we were grasping at fools' gold, and suspected there would be far greater obstacles to overcome, before we could claim the ultimate victory.

Chapter Sixteen

It was the daunting sound of that farmyard cockerel crowing, which brought me out of a cat nap I was enjoying at home, slumped back in an armchair with a small bowl of unattended fruit on my lap. Exhaustion had finally laid its grip on my whole body, following the spate of late hours and over extended mental reasoning. I reached across for my mobile phone and was surprised by the voice on the other end.

Patch Humpage sounded quite anxious, as he suggested we met as soon as I could get down to our usual safe location. In fact, I had never before heard the man sound so unsettled and concerned.

I agreed and after dipping my head into a bowl full of cold water to refresh my faculties, drove away, heading for the city centre and its infamous red-light district.

"There's a new kid on the block, and I don't mean one of the usual vagrants," Patch declared from his bar room stool, at the same time, looking around the room, which was a rarity for him, considering we were in our usual familiar surroundings.

"Go on," I said, encouragingly.

"Word has it, a pro is on the streets, one who is tooled up and engaged in pulling off some hit."

"A contract killer?"

"Yep. I haven't much detail but my source is usually on the button. She can't give me any details other than, he's a geezer and has a Geordie accent."

"From Newcastle?"

"Or thereabouts, but what's interesting is that our man has been commissioned to bump off a cop, and a female cop at that. And we both know there's only one of them likely to fit the frame."

"Have you told your people about this?" I asked, referring to the police.

"Not yet, but I thought you'd best be told first. After what's been happening with Ma'am Goodman, I don't know who to trust in that mob anymore."

"I need to know your source, Patch."

He shook his head, as I'd expected he would, and confirmed, "You've got more chance of reaching the craters on the moon, but I will tell you this much, so you don't think I'm coming across with a load of fanny. She runs what most heavy villains believe is a safe house and is usually the first port of call for visitors to our wonderful city, intent on emptying the bank vaults."

"I take it he was a loner?"

"It seems that way, and again, according to my source, was tooled up. She noticed some kind of rifle case under his bed when she went in to clean his room."

"How does she know it's a female cop?"

He seemed to be hesitant and then confessed, "She noticed a piece of crumpled up paper apparently in the bloke's bin, and saw the words roughly pencilled on it."

I couldn't help but look dubious, and he quickly continued, "I know, that could mean anything, but what's the odds against our lady being set up?"

"How long has he been here, did you find that much out?"

"Couple of days, no more. He's left his digs now but gave her twenty quid on top of his bill. My guess is, he'll still be around, until he's completed his job, that's for sure. Oh, and he dresses in blacks."

It all fitted in with what, Patch was telling me. A loner with a rifle, moving about without spending more than a couple of days in one place. My man's information had to be treated seriously.

"Do me a favour Patch, and call this one in," I suggested, "Even if this geezer's paymaster is a member of your mob, and if he gets wise to someone knowing about his visit here, it might put him off carrying out his contract."

"It might, but won't he just come back at a later time to finish the job?"

Patch had made a good point. It was all about balancing the risk factors. Either we brought in the official police to back us in protecting their former Head of CID, or we put our own ring of steel around, Jean Goodman. But there again, how long could we possibly do that, before the hired killer struck? Also, we would be unarmed, which would still give any potential killer the edge over us. The problem I was faced with, was that if anything did happen to Jean, and we hadn't told the police, I would never be able to forgive myself.

"Call it in, Patch."

Since our girl's initial arrest, she had spent most of her time at home, too distressed and embarrassed to leave her house, except for the occasional excursion with, Malcolm Richards to meet that farcical pretence of a senior officer from London purporting to have been in charge of her case, and of course, to tend to her parents' graves. At least that meant her movements, or rather, restricted movements, limited any attempt on her life. I called a meeting of the full team, to take place at Jean's house the following morning.

When I arrived at the house, thankfully it was a lot earlier than when the meeting had been called for, and my faith in the cops was partially restored, when I found two plain clothes officers sitting with her in her lounge. Both were introduced to me as firearms officers, one an Inspector and the other a Sergeant. I recognised the senior of the two from my days as an active detective. Roger Hausman, was an honest hard working and committed man from my recollection. It was he who briefly explained the threat placed on the lady's well-being, as reported by, Patch Humpage, and of course, I made no mention of having got the same information first hand, the previous evening.

"Do you place much credence on what you've been told?" I asked the Inspector.

"I think we have no other choice, so much so, I was just telling ma'am here, that we think it would be wise to post a couple of firearms operatives, to remain here with her."

"How long for, Roger?" I asked, genuinely hoping there was more to his plan than just playing nurse maid to our girl.

"How long is a piece of string," he answered, "I think we shouldn't look beyond let's say a week and then review it all after that."

In a way I was relieved, knowing that, at least, if a purported killer was to turn up on her doorstep, we would have some shooters available to take him out. But the immediate problem was how to confidentially communicate with Jean, without there being a cop present and within hearing. I suppose I wanted my cake and eat it.

"Will I be able to go out?" Jean asked, as if reading my mind.

"We couldn't stop you," Roger Hausman conceded, "But I would advise you only to leave the house when it was absolutely necessary, until this has been resolved one way or another. I am also going to maintain a firearms mobile crew close to the vicinity during the time my lads remain with you." The man *was* taking the threat seriously, but there again, he would undoubtedly have been aware of the value of any information coming from, Patch Humpage.

One thing was certain, I needed to divert the meeting I had planned with the others, fairly quickly, so offered my apologies, before making for the front door. It was obvious, Jean knew what I was about, but when I stepped out on to the front drive way, the Firearms Inspector was right behind me.

"Might I have a quick word," he begged.

I turned to face him and he made some effort to convince me that there would be no breach of confidentiality should any of his team overhear any conversation connected with Jean's case.

"For what it's worth boss..."

I was once again getting used to being called by that name and assumed that after people knew you as their gaffer for so many years in the past, it was difficult to call you anything else.

"...And you can take this anyway you like, I personally believe ma'am has had a raw deal in all of this. She's been dealt with for all the wrong reasons, and I can assure you there's a lot of us who condemned the isolation policy against her and the manner in which she's been treated."

"Do you think, Roger, she's guilty of having done what they allege?"

"No, not for a second."

"Thank you."

I was pleased to hear his affirmation, but still knew we had to maintain as much secrecy as possible regarding our activities and couldn't afford to give away the slightest indication of anything we planned. In other words, the lines had been drawn and I certainly had no intention of crossing them, no matter how much I might have trusted an individual. Patch Humpage was different, and my faith in him, had already paid dividends.

As soon as I had driven away from Jean's house, I quickly rang the others and arranged the meeting to take place at our usual safe location, in the city centre bar, but before leaving the district altogether, I stopped and turned back. It was more on impulse that I felt the need to take a quick look at the immediate area surrounding Jean's house. left my car around the corner from my girl's home and walked back. When I got close to the same driveway I had just had that short conversation with Roger Hausman, I stopped and looked around.

The back of the house was fairly secure, with a garden fence backing on to a public right of way, which made it virtually impossible for anyone to secrete themselves. At the front, and right opposite, Jean's house was a high brick wall on the opposite side of the street, which again, immediately ruled out any likely sniper position. The same high wall continued up the street and turned left into another side road, confirming that the left-hand side of that thoroughfare, as you faced Jean's house, was a fairly safe location from which it would have been virtually impossible for anyone to remain concealed. Further down and away from the house, on the same opposite side, were the upper levels of the backs of other houses. I immediately determined it was from there, any sniper would favour, because one particular bedroom window afforded visual access into the front of the target's house.

Having decided to knock on a few doors on the pretext of asking where the local shops were, there were three domiciles that came into contention. Two of them, I quickly confirmed were lived in by families, but the third was empty, having been recently sold and was awaiting the new buyers to move in. The back-bedroom window of that particular house would be perfect for anyone wishing to look through Jean's front window, directly into her lounge. It was the only possible location, unless the gunman was capable of seeing through brick walls.

I quickly returned and told the two firearms lads of what I had discovered, but much to my pleasant surprise they were already aware, and in fact, the Inspector confirmed he had already posted two of his armed officers up there, just in case. I was duly impressed and told them so.

Our meeting was brief, and although the team produced more information concerning recent operations involving Jean Goodman, and a detailed dossier on, Robert Snipe's background and service history, there was nothing which attracted my attention. So, I decided to put most of my eggs into one basket, and told them about the news I had been given by Laser Johnson, that one of Julie Roberts customers was a serving cop. We desperately needed to identify that particular punter and decided to focus entirely on doing just that, by making enquiries with other prostitutes in the district, including even publicans who lived within the shadows of the red-light district.

Obviously, I mentioned the recent threat to Jean Goodman's life and the fact that firearms officers would from now on be present at her home address.

The news surprised them all, and for a moment of silence, they all looked at each in bewilderment.

Then it was Neil Rowbotham who remarked, "How much bloody more can that lady be expected to take?"

"Well, we can ask the bastard who started all of this, once we get our hands on him," I answered.

After leaving my group of dedicated performers, I immediately rang, Malcolm Richards and updated him on the recent events, before suggesting he might need to put in an appearance with Jean, at least until things had settled down. I also made inference to her brother, Raymond, suggesting he be told of what was taking place, not wanting to panic the man, but I thought it was only right he was made fully aware, although it would be more beneficial if he remained absent from his sister's house, for the time being in any case. He could always phone her.

Within a minute of returning to my car, that bloody cockerel sounded off again, and I could see it was, Dave Collins, my editor on the other end. That was the last thing I needed at that particular moment, but he was paying my wages, so I guessed it was only right I spoke to the man.

Chapter Seventeen

After the exigencies of that morning, my mind was still locked into the goings on at Jean's house. In fairness to my editor, the paper I was working for had been very good in supporting, the former Head of CID and asking pertinent questions of the police, but he still felt the need for an update. I agreed to meet him in the city centre later that afternoon.

In more propitious circumstances, I would never have held anything back, and although I did quickly brief him on recent events, I missed out details of the firearms threat to the lady's life. In fact, he was surprisingly, understanding and empathetic towards where we were at, and actually proposed that I should be guided by how things panned out, which was what I was planning to do in any case. After a couple of beers, it was early evening by the time I left my editor in a city centre public house, not far from the newspaper building, and instantly made my way across to, Jean Goodman's domicile.

I had almost forgotten about the company she was keeping these days, until one of the armed officers answered the door. Knowing who I was, he just nodded and stepped aside to allow me access, and I found the lady of the house sitting in her lounge with the second officer. I also noticed that all the curtains had been drawn, although it was still fairly light outside, but I understood the need not to expose, Jean as an easy target. Although she smiled and was putting on a brave face, she still looked tired and drawn. Neil Rowbotham had been right to ask, how much more could, Jean Goodman be expected to take, and I was beginning to ask the same question to myself.

"Did Malcolm call in to see you earlier?" I asked, referring to her welfare representative.

"Yes, but I told him to go home. He has been spending a lot of time away, looking after me and I thought he was beginning to look a little tired."

No more than how she was looking, I thought.

She also confirmed that her brother had rang and had been advised to stay away, until the current situation had been resolved one way or another. Although the lady's current predicament could go on for a number of days, possibly weeks, I suspected, whatever move was being planned against her, would take place sooner rather than later.

According to Patch Humpage, the man with the Geordie accent had left his first safe house, so was on the loose somewhere. I envisaged, as soon as he had prepared his ground, he would attempt his strike. From my own limited experience of professional contract killers, I was aware they usually travelled around on motor bikes and would have a second machine available close by, following the hit, and in reserve in case something happened to their preferred ride. I was tempted to share that knowledge with the firearms lads, but there again, thought they would deem it as being intrusive on their operation. But that hadn't stopped me from looking for a motor bike parked up, as I had approached the street in which, Jean lived.

I then asked how she was feeling after the committal proceedings, and she told me she was trying her best to take everything in her stride. We then continued with some small talk, knowing that there were police officers there with us.

Jean came across as being confident, but I knew it was only a courageous act put on for the benefit of her bodyguards.

Then one of them stood from the seat he was occupying, and I watched him, knowing he was receiving some information over his earpiece.

He then spoke into a small microphone attached to his shirt and asked, "Front or back?"

Turning to his mate, he asked, "Did you get all of that, Steve."

"Affirmative," his mate confirmed, "I'll do it. You stay here with ma'am Goodman."

I watched the lad produce his hand weapon, a Magnum, as he switched off the lights in the lounge before making for the door.

The officer left behind, turned and suggested we lay down on the floor just to be safe, explaining that a suspect was approaching the void house across the way, in which firearms officers were covertly waiting.

We both did as we had been advised, and I just hoped and prayed the suspect mentioned was the man we were seeking. It would be a great relief to get this particular monkey off our backs.

With the curtain remaining closed, the lounge was virtually in complete darkness, and I could see no harm in crawling up to the front window and cautiously peering through a crack in the curtain.

"I wouldn't do that if I was you, sir," the armed lad suggested.

"You're not me," I quietly snapped back at him.

Jean remained sitting on the floor, well away from the window, with her back resting against one of the soft chairs, and I could see a hint of apprehension in her eyes.

Looking down the street, I watched as the lad who had just left us, was leaning up against the tall wall which ran along the opposite side. There was no sign of any firearm, and he seemed as though he was waiting to meet somebody. Then it all suddenly came together, as a second man appeared, walking towards Jean's house, but still on the opposite side of the road, and approaching the armed policeman who remained leaning against the wall.

The officer who was still inside the house, standing behind me, was obviously listening to what was going on through his earpiece, and quickly produced his own handgun, before moving towards the door. He opened it ajar but remained inside the hallway.

When the newcomer on the scene reached a streetlight, I could see he was carrying some kind of holdall in one hand.

Our man then made his move, springing out, away from the wall and grasping his handgun with both hands, pointing the barrel directly at the man with the holdall.

I heard him scream out, "Armed police, drop the case, now," just as two other officers, both pointing guns in the direction of the odd man out, seemed to appear from nowhere. The target was caught in the middle of the three-armed officers.

He then turned away from the first gun and crouched down, facing the wall, dropping the holdall to the pavement. But then, as if feeling an urge to commit suicide, he straightened up with a handgun of his own within his grasp.

A total of six shots were fired, none of which missed their target, before the gunman had time to raise the barrel of his pistol. He immediately collapsed to the ground, and I overheard our man who was still watching from the hallway, quickly summon an ambulance over his radio, whilst the officers responsible for bringing the would-be killer down, gathered all around his lifeless body.

It had happened all so quickly, and forgetting I was no longer one of their number, turned to, Jean and said, "It's okay. It's all over," before running from the house and across the road. But before I reached the small group still standing over the gunned down man, one of them turned and shouted at me to stand back.

"Go back to where you came from," the young firearms officer ordered, "This is now a crime scene."

Of course, it was, I was forgetting myself in the heat of the moment. And as I retraced my steps, thinking I should have known better, it began to rain cats and dogs.

It later transpired that very little information came from the dead man. He carried nothing from which he could be identified, and both fingerprint and odontology tests were having to be made in an effort to at least discover a name. What did label him however, as being a professional contract killer, was a high-powered rifle with a telescopic sight and ammunition found inside the holdall he had been carrying. The firearms lads had recovered a Beretta 92 revolver from the ground near to where he had fallen, a popular weapon used by a number of contract killers.

Although, the failure to snuff out, Jean Goodman had failed miserably, there was a real possibility that whoever it was who wanted her dead, might just send another assassin to finish the job. Of course, I didn't tell her that but knew very well, we would all have to remain extra vigilant from then on. What I was now more convinced of than ever before, was that the need to track down the person behind all of this, had suddenly become an absolutely top priority. Whoever it was we sought, had shown his cards to us. He was a desperate individual, considering the extremes he had already gone to. I was convinced that Jean herself, had the answer. She had something; some item or knowledge that was capable of bringing our tormentor down. But what? We had gone over just about every possibility without success. Then, as if providence had taken a hand, we had our first meaningful break, thanks to yet another call I received later that night from, guess who? Patch Humpage.

When I arrived to find him propping up the bar, I was stunned to see none other than, Laser Johnson's number one girl, Roberta Cummings, perched on a stool next to him. The girl was staring down at a large glass of her usual preference; Pernod and Lemonade.

Patch was smiling and winked an eye at me, provoking me into thinking that he already knew about the result at, Jean Goodman's house. I wasn't surprised in the least.

"She wants to say a few words to you," he declared, nodding towards the professional night worker.

When she lifted her head, I was shocked to see in the dim light, a number of heavy bruises below both eyes, and a slight trickle of dried blood from her nose. She had been badly beaten, and you didn't have to be a super sleuth to guess who had been responsible.

I could physically feel anger climbing through the roof, as I asked, "Where is he, Bobby?"

Patch answered for the girl and quickly told me that, Johnson would soon be found and sorted out by a few heavies who were opposed to seeing any girl bullied by little men who just used them to fill their own pockets.

"Before you came in though, Bobby was just telling me that she intends changing her occupation and was thinking about going back to teaching."

That was the second shock I had received, since walking in through the door. Never in all the years I had spent working the streets, had I ever known of a teacher becoming a prostitute. But as the wide boys who are forced to reduce the cost of their wares, to sell them in the open markets can often be heard saying, 'Why not?'

"Where had you used to teach, Bobby?" I calmly and respectfully asked the lady, who now appeared to have taken on a whole completely different character since we had last met.

"Only at primary level, but I've earned enough money now to ensure my little girl can go all the way through private school, so it's time to return to respectability." She didn't smile, because I didn't think she could. It would have been too painful. The reason why she was giving up the game was obvious, and who could blame her. The next time her bullying pimp decided to use her as a punchbag, might be her last, or she could finish up in a wheelchair.

"Let him have that parting shot you were telling me about," Patch said, "Before I start crying."

I wouldn't have thought that half human, half sewer rat, whose body odour was offensive to even the lowest of the low, had a tear inside his head, but waited patiently for the girl to continue talking to me.

"And you swear he isn't old bill?" she asked my former colleague, with obvious concern, and obviously not knowing his true identity.

"How many times have I got to tell yer. Would I be mixing around with him, if he was."

Patch then looked at me, and asked, "Which newspaper do you work for?"

"The Weekend Chronicle," I instantly answered.

"See?" Patch said, looking again at the girl.

She nodded, before telling me that the murdered girl, Julie Roberts, had quite a lengthy list of clients from various walks of life and with various perversions. But there was one, the dead girl had spoken of to, Bobby, on a number of occasions, who used to enjoy beating up on her that much, he paid over the odds for his depraved pleasures.

"You see, Julie found herself in the middle of the Devil and the deep blue sea, in that, she no longer wanted anything to do with this particular customer, because he was becoming too violent towards her, yet, Laser refused to allow her to give the bloke the cold shoulder, as he always paid good money and plenty of it."

"Did she ever mention his name, Bobby," I asked quietly.

She shook her head and told me that a name had never been mentioned.

"But she did tell me he was a copper and that she thought he was one of the big noises. She once told me how, on one occasion, whilst he was sleeping in her bed, she managed to go through his wallet, and took a few more quid for her troubles. But she also mentioned she'd noticed an address on a folded envelope inside the wallet, which was in Northampton."

"Without there being any name above that address?"

"I don't know, that's all she told me. She couldn't even remember the address because it wasn't important to her at the time, but she did recall Northampton being a part of it."

At least it was something for us to bear in mind, as I was becoming more convinced that there was every possibility this man who beat up on his women, could have been the killer. It takes a lot for any man, to place his hands around someone else's throat and strangle them to death. Unlike killing a person with a bullet, or blowing them up from a distance, the act of strangulation requires the killer to get close to his victim, which would put most afflicted perverts off.

I thanked the lady for her help by slipping a twenty-pound note, surreptitiously into her palm, as I kissed her on the cheek and wished her well, once she had returned to her former life. Then, after patting the undercover lad on the shoulder and having his reassurance that, Laser Johnson would get his full just desserts, I left them huddled together over the bar.

As I drove home that night I could sense a prevailing mood of optimism, and felt somewhat elated by the realisation, that finally, I believed we were getting closer to our man. It had been quite a day and I was in desperate need of sleep and rest, but a principle suspect had already come to mind, although I wasn't ready just then, to inform the rest of the world. There was a warm and comfortable bed awaiting my presence, before doing that.

Chapter Eighteen

She was remarkably calm, considering what had taken place outside the front of her house on the evening before. Her neighbours must have thought they were living in the Wild West. As soon as I landed at Jean Goodman's home the following morning, the questions flew at me like bullets from an automatic machine gun.

"Do they know who he is yet?"

"Have you any idea who sent him?"

"Whereabouts did he come from?"

"Had I ever met him before?" And so on, and so forth.

I answered what few I could, but obviously the information I shared with the lady was sparse. But that wasn't the reason I was there. I needed to talk further about the, Jean Roberts murder. She unknowingly had a secret locked away in that head of hers, and I was absolutely determined to extract it.

"I need you to think back and tell me if you can remember the very last thing you did on that Inquiry?" We were sitting facing each other in the lounge, and Malcolm Richards was also present, having already listened to the events involving the Firearms lads. The usual pot of tea had been made, and Jean appeared to be much more receptive than she had been for some time.

"I signed the lads overtime forms," she answered, looking a bit bewildered, probably by the way in which I had approached the subject with so much urgency.

"No, I mean at the scene of the murder."

Pensively she sat there, trying hard to recollect, exactly what action she had taken.

"I had already identified the lines of enquiry we should follow, arranged for the house to house calls to be made, and confirmed the motive wasn't theft, as nothing seemed to be missing from the flat." She was counting off each point she made on her fingers and paused for a moment to recollect her thoughts further, and then added, "Oh, and I can remember asking for the registered owners list to be treated with some urgency."

"What list was that?"

"The caretaker who lived at number one Grimshaw House. We spoke to him and at first, I thought he was a seedy character, who might turn out to be a suspect. He was one of those who had eyes everywhere and initially, kept appearing outside the murdered victim's flat trying to prise information from the detectives. Anyway, it transpired he was just being nosy, and we found out he had kept a list of car numbers belonging to customers who frequently visited Julie Roberts."

I could not believe what I was hearing.

"Were the enquiries into that list ever completed?" I asked with enthusiasm.

"No, I had to leave it with the Incident Room staff to deal with, as I was taken off the case just after that."

"What was the reason for you being moved away?"

"Some intelligence came in about a terrorist bomb threat and they needed someone to liaise with the security forces. As you know, I was one of the few who had clearance to do that."

"Can you remember how soon after you left the Julie Roberts Inquiry, did those vultures come calling here and arrest you?"

"Two weeks, no more. I was still dealing with the people from Whitehall at the time. It was papers relating to those inquiries I was worried about making secure, when Snipe and his people landed here."

"I've got them," Malcolm Richards confirmed, "As soon as, Jean, told me, I took possession of them and they are securely locked away in my safe at home."

I sat back, with both of them staring at me inquisitively. Then I calmly asked, "Do we know where that list of vehicles is now?"

"I can only presume it will be with whichever officer was tasked with tracing the registered owners."

I looked across at, Malcolm, reluctant to ask the man to put his own neck at risk but knowing it would virtually have been impossible for me to recover that list, which I was so desperate to see by then, I asked, "Is there any chance you could make some enquiries covertly, Malcolm, to try and find its current whereabouts?"

He looked across at Jean and quietly said, "I don't see why not. I could make some excuse up for visiting the Incident Room to see what I can turn up. Who's the officer in charge of that room, Jean?"

"It was Inspector Taylor, Gordon Taylor. I'm not sure if he's still there."

"I know him well," Malcolm remarked.

"Can you trust him?" I enquired.

"No," the welfare representative abruptly answered, "But I'm sure I can get what information I need from him. Leave it to me."

Things were beginning to move at a pace now, and I was anxious to visit the caretaker at the block of flats where, Julie Roberts had lived, but first needed to speak with, Sandra Jenson and, Rolly Guthrie. I arranged to meet them both at our usual safe location.

At the same time as I was leaving, Jean's house, Malcolm Richards was about to escort the lady for a walk, at her request. I had been impressed by the Chief Superintendent's dedication to the lady throughout the Inquiry, and was in no doubt that what little, Malcolm didn't know about the caring welfare of others, wasn't worth knowing.

"Don't look so worried," were the words I greeted my hard working and loyal colleagues with, before buying each of them a mineral water, including myself.

"We've managed to compile background dossiers on most of those senior officers involved in the, Jean Chapman case, and there doesn't seem to be anything that might have been of interest to us," Rolly explained.

"Except, for what it's worth, on the DCC," Sandra added, "Before transferring up here, he worked in the Metropolitan Police for a period of six years. During that time, he instigated the dismissal of eleven women."

"That's a lot of female staff in six years," I remarked.

"Each one of them took him to an Industrial Tribunal."

"Were any of them successful?"

"No, but the interesting thing is that they were all women and of Asian origin."

I sat in silence for a brief moment, digesting that information, before Sandra continued, "The reason given for all of their dismissals over that same period, was that they were neglectful in the jobs they were doing."

"It doesn't prove much though," I said, "Especially as they had all of their cases thrown out by the Tribunal."

"It goes to show he doesn't like women much though," Rolly sarcastically pointed out, with a grin on his face.

"Maybe," I answered insincerely, "But the reason I wanted this meeting with you both is, we need to concentrate more on the Julie Roberts case."

"The murdered prostitute."

"Yes, there was a list of vehicle registration numbers handed in to the Major Incident Room, and I need to know if anything was done about them?"

"Whether they were entered on to the system?" Sandra suggested.

"Exactly. Is there anyway either of you could find out?"

They both looked at each with blank expressions. Then Sandra explained that she could find out, if she could get access into the computer system, "But that would mean having to get into the Incident Room itself."

"Not necessarily," Rolly explained, "The data base in the Incident Room is a slave terminal, networked to the main frame which is kept at Police Headquarters, in a small office adjacent to the main control room. I spent a few weeks up there once, doing penal servitude after dropping in the shit. It might be possible to gain access from there."

"How?" I asked.

"Well, unlike the Incident Room, there is no alarm system, and if we visited at night when there aren't many people about, we might be able to pull it off."

"What about any intrusion being identified. Wouldn't they know it was you who'd been into the system?"

Rolly smiled. "No, don't worry, I've done it before and have a bag of tricks for preventing just that."

"And what if you're caught?"

"Then we'll have a contingency plan to explain what we were doing there. It's worth a try."

Such a haphazard proposal didn't really surprise me. It was because of fraught situations such as this, I had recruited, Rolly and the others in the first place.

"Let me know how it goes," I said before leaving them.

My next port of call was, Grimshaw House and I quickly found number one flat on the ground floor. There was a group of unruly kids making some noise in the foyer but ignoring them, I hammered on the door.

Gordon Taylor was a small, rounded man with thinning hair and a pair of rimless spectacles covering his nose. He was wearing a grey jumper over a grey shirt, when he answered the door, which was surprising as the temperature outside had risen considerably since the early morning. His whole appearance reminded me of one of those stalkers who nicked women's clothing off washing lines.

I introduced myself as a reporter from the paper I in fact worked for, and he responded with an excited voice and eyes resembling a Hollywood extra having just been offered an extended contract.

I told the man that we were looking at running a story about the murder that had taken place upstairs and asked if he wouldn't mind having his photograph in the papers at a later time.

Obviously, Christmas morning had come early and the caretaker jumped at the opportunity of injecting some fame into, what would have been a fairly dull existence.

"What can you tell me about it Mr. Taylor?" I asked, preferring he disclosed the existence of the list of vehicles without being prompted.

"She was a prostitute," he offered.

"Yes, I'm aware of that."

"It was dreadful. One of her punters strangled the life out of the poor girl."

"What makes you think it was one of her customers?" I asked.

"It was obvious. Who else would have done that to that poor wretched girl." There was still no mention of the list of registration numbers, and I could see, he was getting more excited just talking about the incident. I asked if he knew the victim at all?

"Yes, I knew her." He paused to look over his shoulder, obviously to make sure his wife or some other person was not within hearing distance. He then whispered, holding a hand to his mouth, "She used to look after me."

"In what way, Mr. Taylor?"

"You know; we're all men of the world, and if she ever wanted a pipe fixing, or door re-painted, I was her man."

"You carried out odd-jobs for her, free of charge, is that what you're telling me?" I knew exactly where the weasel was coming from, but needed it to come from the horse's mouth, as it were.

"Not for free, if you follow me. She used to look after me on occasions, in kind you might say." The devious look on his face, signalling a willingness to boast about his sexual prowess was nauseating, so I decided to push the interview along a bit.

"Any idea who might have killed her?" I asked.

He shook his head, and moved closer, assaulting my nostrils with his garlic smelling breath.

"I've already given details of the killer to the police."

"Oh, you do know who killed her then?"

"It was one of a few who used to visit her for favours. I wrote down the numbers of their cars each time they came and told the police."

"Blimey, you could get some kind of a bravery award then?"

He seemed please at the suggestion, and continued, "I suppose I could, after they've caught him."

"I have an idea of how to let the public know just what kind of a hero you are. Have you got a copy of that list?" It was a long shot and quickly proved to be just that.

"No," he said, "I gave it to the police, but they did say they would get back to me and seemed very pleased with the help I'd given them."

"What about any descriptions of these men. Did you give any to the police?"

"I did, and the one detective commented on how methodical I'd been."

"Tell me, was one of Julie Roberts visitors a small, pale faced man, with short dark brown hair?"

"Could have been; there were a few that looked like that."

Momentarily, I wondered if the caretaker was making it all up, just to get some attention. Anyway, our meeting was abruptly ended when a woman's voice called out from inside his flat, telling, 'Gordon', his tea was on the table.

I smiled and left him, not really enthusiastic about returning. I had no doubt the man had provided some genuine information concerning the dead girl's punters but wouldn't want him to be the only witness upon whose evidence a life sentence was dished out. I needed to see that list of vehicles he'd handed over to the police, and more importantly, I needed to know if any action had been taken to progress it further, that was if it still existed. I had my doubts and could only hope that either, Malcolm Richards, or Rolly Guthrie and, Sandra Jenson came up trumps.

Chapter Nineteen

They both looked as if they hadn't slept for a week, instead of just one night, and just sat there obviously dejected and showing all the signs of sleep deprivation.

I sat down opposite and placed my cup of coffee on top of the table, waiting for one of them to speak first. It was Rolly.

"Sorry, but we couldn't find it," he solemnly confessed, "We went through the whole data base but there was no list of motor vehicles anywhere to be found. Are we certain one existed?"

"According to, Jean Goodman, there was."

"Well, there's no reason why there shouldn't have been a record of it on that database. I can only assume it's got lost somewhere in amongst the documents in the Incident Room, and nobody's got round to inputting it on to the system, yet."

"Or it's disappeared," Sandra suggested.

I nodded towards the girl and then proposed they didn't get too down hearted.

"If that list has disappeared, what does that tell us?" I asked them both.

"That someone has deliberately got rid of it."

"Exactly, and by doing that, it means a vehicle registered to whoever has disposed of it, might very well have been included on it. You see, if we look at the absence of what could have been damning evidence towards identifying the killer positively, it does indicate that the killer was a client of the dead girl, and that he travelled to the scene, and probably left in a vehicle. Also, by that same list of car numbers having disappeared, then it could only have been a serving cop who was responsible. So, the work you did last night as accomplished a number of facts for us."

"I never thought of it like that," Rolly remarked, "Perhaps that's the reason why somebody has tried their best to get rid of ma'am Goodman, because there was a danger that she would have found out the identity of the killer from that same list," he surmised.

"Now you are thinking along the same lines as myself."

"But why attempt to destroy her, if the killer had already removed the evidence that could have identified him?" Sandra asked.

"What if, Jean Goodman had kept a copy of that same list?" I suggested.

"Has she?" Rolly asked, enthusiastically.

"No, but the killer wouldn't know that."

"Is there anything more we can do?" Sandra asked.

I just sat there pondering over the lady's plea to help further. If that list of vehicles had been destroyed, which appeared to be highly likely now, it was gone and there was nothing we could do to retrieve it. But, apart from a very unreliable caretaker, if the killer was the same man behind, Jean's series of traumatic events and had also been a client of Julie Roberts, somebody must have seen him, when visiting that flat. There was no chance of the prostitute's pimp, Laser Johnson speaking to us, and it might just be, by that time, he was lying at the bottom of some ditch covered in rocks as a result of what he had lashed out on Roberta Cummings.

"I need a photograph of Adrian Plum," I suddenly blurted out.

"We could arrange that without much problem," Rolly confirmed, "But don't tell me you suspect the DCC of being a murderer."

I didn't answer, because I wasn't sure whether Plum was the kind of man to commit murder. He was certainly the type to cause enough grief to a senior female officer though, sufficient for her to attempt to commit suicide. But that was different, and to even think of accusing the man without some hard, factual evidence, would be cataclysmic for all involved. Apart from that, he would only deny it, at the same time as his solicitors prepared the papers for commencing legal proceedings for defamation.

"Get me the snapshot and twenty or so copies of it, and then we shall all start visiting a few doors in that block of flats."

Malcolm Richards was already waiting for me at Jean's house when I arrived. He was looking as dejected as the couple I had just left in the city.

"Tell me you managed to recover that list of vehicles," I begged, but he just shook his head, before explaining.

"No one working in that incident room, has ever caught sight of it. It's as if it has never existed."

I turned to, Jean and asked, "You definitely saw it personally?"

"I took it off the caretaker," she said, confidently.

"Then we can only assume someone has got rid of it." I then told them about my suspicions concerning, Adrian Plum, and they both found it hard to accede to my way of thinking. I continued to explain what my plan of action was, to show the DCC's photograph to a few of the neighbours living in the tower block, and again they looked at me dubiously.

"Are we going to do the same with Tony Freer?" Jean enquired, referring to the Assistant Chief Constable responsible for physically suspending her from duty, "Should not all senior officers be suspected?"

"Why not," I answered, "But do you really think that such an incompetent man as Freer, could be capable of committing murder and then plan to bring you down in the manner in which they have?"

"No," said Malcolm Richards, "But I've always thought Plum had a nasty streak and concur that he could be a suspect. How are you going to get a photograph of him?"

"That shouldn't be a problem," I explained, "My lot will just wait until he appears out of Police Headquarters and snap him."

"I've got a better idea," he said, going on to explain that he had a group photograph which contained himself and the DCC taken at some social event the year before.

"He's also wearing a normal suit and tie in that picture, which might be safer showing it to members of the public, than one which would identify him as a police officer, and a senior one at that."

The man had a point, and I asked if he could get copies of the same photograph with just, Adrian Plum's face on it?

He agreed and told me he would return later that day with a few copies to show around.

I immediately got hold of, Rolly Guthrie and told him to hold back with his camera, until I made contact with him later.

Jean's solicitor, John Mitchell, then rang her, whilst we were still at the house, and told her the case had been listed for the following month, which gave us three weeks before the commencement of the trial. Time was short, and I wondered whether it had been wise putting all our eggs into one basket, by linking the prostitute's murder with the, Jean Goodman case. But the more I dwelled on the circumstances of both Inquiries, the more I was convinced there was some form of conjugation between the two incidents.

Outside, the day was bright and sunny, so I decided to take a car journey across country to an adjacent police force, whilst Malcolm returned home to carry out his tasks relevant to the DCC's photograph, and Jean drove herself to visit her parents' graves. Although on the surface, she remained stable in appearance, I remained wary those psychological gremlins could soon return, as we got closer to the commencement of her trial. But for now, it was pleasing to see some of her old bounce and confidence being displayed.

I had known, Phil Gardiner since we were young Detective Sergeants together, and our paths had occasionally crossed throughout what, Phil had enjoyed as an illustrious career. He had now reached the dizzy height of holding down the rank of Chief Constable in an adjoining county force. A tall man, well over six foot, slim with a youthful fresh clean-shaven face and a good sense of humour, he was also extremely trustworthy and I knew I could regard him as a confidante. In the same way as with, Jean Goodman, we had shared a great number of successful operational adventures in the past, the kind of perilous situations which tended to bond people together for a long time to come.

Having reached the large mansion, standing in its own expansive grounds, and which was the Police Headquarters, where local training was also prominent, I asked to see my old friend, and was told to wait. After a short period, a young Inspector approached me and confirmed the Chief Constable was free and would see me. I was delighted.

Phil hadn't changed a bit, except he was now housed in an office that was bigger than all the rooms in my house put together. He was standing in his shirt and trousers when I was shown in, and immediately welcomed me with his usual vice like grip, which I'd forgotten about.

"Tea, coffee or something stronger?" he enquired.

"Tea would be just fine," I answered, appreciatively.

"It is good to see you after all of these years, but I hear you have now retired," he mentioned, as we both took seats on either side of a large ornamental fireplace. The walls inside that vast room were covered in portraits of past Chief Constables, and former Lieutenants of the County, in all their brightly coloured regalia. A large oak carved desk stood in front of a ceiling to floor window, giving the impression it had been there since the early nineteenth century mansion house had been built in the Greek Revival style.

I briefly told him what I was doing in an attempt to make a living and he quipped, "I'm not surprised you are a writer, remembering all that bullshit you used to feed old Knuckle Head and Jones the Olympic Torch, with." He was referring to our own senior detectives of years gone by, and we both laughed.

"So, what brings this city gent out to our peaceful and serene neck of the woods? Don't tell me you are looking at reviewing an historical murder or the such like?"

"No, it's nothing like that, Phil," I said, and went on to explain my involvement in the, Jean Goodman case.

"Ah," he said, lowering his voice, "I heard all about that. A bit harsh I thought. I remember, Jean when she was a young attached girl with excellent promise and wasn't surprised when they eventually made her Head of CID."

At that, the tea arrived on a tray filled with best china cups and a teapot that resembled an urn. Biscuits on a plate were also included, and I waited for the young girl who had brought them in, to leave. Then, out of respect to my high-ranking friend, I got straight to the point.

"What do you know of, Adrian Plum, the DCC over there?"

My host raised the fingers of both hands to form a pyramid beneath his chin and quietly, almost reluctantly asked, "What is it you wish to know about him?"

From the look in Phil's eyes, I detected a hint of resentment, so pushed the boat out.

"How well do you know him, and I would value your confidential opinion as to his character."

The Chief Constable blew his cheeks out and rolled his eyes. Then he asked, "Do you want a truthful answer, or one which could be used in some article you are writing?"

"I did mention, in confidence."

"Very well. I have met your man on several occasions at various inter-force liaisons and a couple of social gatherings. Adrian Plum is typical of the younger breed of Chief Officers today, unfortunately."

"In what way?"

"He's extremely ambitious, which isn't a bad thing, but he is also very self-confident which crosses the border into being arrogant. He is also, in my view mind you, dishonest, which is taboo when performing at such a high level within the hierarchy. I believe he came from the Met, where he must have picked up most of his bad habits, but before that he was in the Northampton Force, where I think he was born and raised."

Northampton? Now where had I heard that being mentioned recently. Wasn't it, Roberta Cummings who had told me that, Julie Roberts, the murdered prostitute, had told her she had seen an envelope bearing a Northampton address?

"Do you know if he still resides there, in Northampton?"

"I've no idea. What is your interest in the man?"

I took a long, deep breath and then asked, "Do you think, Adrian Plum is capable of murder?"

"Heaven forbid, I would hate to think I thought of any serving police officer as being capable of murder. Do you think he is?"

"I don't know, but every question I ask about the man seems to indicate that he could very well be."

I reached over to pour the tea, leaving my host to consider further the opinion I had just thrown at him, like a pointed lance.

"Does the force know about these assertions?" he then asked.

"No, I can't afford to share anything with them at the moment."

"I understand. Well, let me give you a piece of advice from an old friend and colleague. If you ever reach a point where you feel it is necessary to take some kind of action against the man we have been discussing, promise you will come to me first, for your own sake and safety."

I looked him in the eyes, and with a broad grin, declared, "That Phil, is exactly the reason I am here."

"I mean it my old friend. There might well be a point where some kind of an independent Inquiry is sought, and I would hate to miss out on that one."

"I appreciate the offer and suspect that might come much sooner than later."

Chapter Twenty

As the date for Jean's trial drew closer, the lady's presence at the Inns of Court in London became more frequent, attending various meetings and conferences with, John Mitchell and her defending counsel. Malcolm Richards continued to support, Jean and never reneged on his responsibility to remain at her side throughout. At least, such excursions and the overall planning of her defence was keeping her mind occupied, which had to be a good thing.

For my part, I arranged for copies of the photograph provided by, Malcolm, to be printed off and the full team was engaged in knocking on doors in the tower block where, Julie Roberts used to reside. In fact, it was on the very first day we began our house to house enquires that we struck gold. Of course, we weren't the first people to conduct such a tactic at that particular venue, police officers having gone before us when making their initial enquiries. But we had photographs to show and help jog the memories of any potential witnesses, which gave us an advantage over our predecessors. My people were also more highly skilled at probing for information than the current crop of detectives and were obviously far more skilled and experienced.

Julie had lived on the eighth floor of the tower block. On the seventh floor, and in the flat immediately below the murdered girl's, lived a young single woman who was busy raising two toddlers. Janet Luft, was not much older than what, Julie Roberts had been, and over a period of a few months had befriended the dead prostitute.

It was, Andy Greatrix and, Dave Stewart who first called me to the flat on the seventh floor, obviously eager for me to join them. When I got there, Janet Luft was standing in the doorway of her residence, with both men standing on each side. The young lady appeared nervous about allowing strange men into her home, and who could blame her, considering the area in which she lived. I could also see signs of continuing grieving over the prostitute's death, in the form of some discolouration around her eyes, the kind resulting from a great deal of weeping.

"Tell us again, Janet, what you know about some of Julie's customers," Andy calmly suggested, repeating an earlier request.

"I was just telling these two gentlemen that you wouldn't come across a more gentler soul than my friend upstairs. Sometimes she would sit in here with me and we would have a cup of tea and a good chat. On other occasions, Julie would invite me into her flat where we would do the same."

"Tell him about those two particular customers you just mentioned to us," Andy insisted, his enthusiastic ardour being obvious.

"Well, I didn't see that much of them. It was only on a couple of occasions I laid eyes on that couple. The first time was when I had to leave Julie's flat, because two men came calling. At the time, I didn't give them a second glance, until, a few days later, one of them returned on his own, whilst I was in there drinking tea. So, again I left, and later that same day, she came to visit me, only she was in tears, having been beaten black and blue. I was shocked and my heart went out to her."

"Did she tell you which of them had beaten up on her?" I calmly asked.

She shook her head. "No, but she didn't have to. It was obvious because on the first occasion, when they were together, she told me then how one of them was into using violence against her to get his kicks. And he was the same man who returned on his own, just before I saw the result of his perverted activity."

"And there were two of them you say?"

"Only on that first occasion when I was in the flat with her. On the second occasion, the smaller one came on his own."

"Can you describe them to us?"

Andy butted in again, stating, "She can do better than that; tell him Janet; you won't be in any trouble, I promise."

She looked at me nervously, and then explained that the murdered girl, Julie, had told her that the smaller of the two, who had an inclination towards violence, was from Northampton, and his name was Adrian Plum.

"She said she was afraid of him but couldn't do nothing because he was high up in the police."

Talk about having just opened up a gold mine. I glanced across at the two lads standing there, who both smiled, and I knew exactly what was in their minds.

Trying to remain calm, I then asked if her friend had mentioned the name of the other, taller man, who had accompanied the first customer on the initial occasion she saw them.

"No, but when I was leaving on that first occasion, I had to pass them in the hallway and the short one said to the other, "Make way for the lady, Tony."

I would have put my very last shilling on, Tony, being none other than, Anthony Freer, the man with the wide girth who had made such a cock up when first trying to suspend, Jean Goodman.

I turned to the two lads and asked, "Has she seen the photograph?" referring to the blow up of Adrian Plum.

"Yep, it was that which brought this lot out into the open," Andy explained, "That's how she recognised him as having visited Julie's flat."

"I knew him straight away," she confirmed, "A horrible, horrible man."

So, that was it. Both Plum and Freer, it appeared, had tried to cover up the murder of a prostitute they were both involved with. In doing so, they had obviously, Plum in particular, looked upon, Jean Goodman, as being a threat to them, especially when she recovered that list of vehicles compiled by the caretaker downstairs. In an effort to get rid of the Head of CID they had gone to an enormous amount of trouble to frame her, and it must have been like pennies from heaven, when the Graingers turned up to complain about the fictitious activities of, Jean. I had no doubt, they both leapt at the opportunity to destroy her, and would have probably succeeded if it hadn't been for the protective ring thrown around her by close friends and former colleagues.

Adrian Plum must have had some reason to believe, Jean had retained a copy of the caretaker's list of vehicles, thinking that the number of his own vehicle was on it. Why else would he be so determined, not just to destroy her career, but it now appeared, was obviously behind the introduction of a paid assassin to finish the job for him.

We needed a full and detailed statement from this courageous young mother of two, and I told Andy to obtain one from the lady, before wholeheartedly thanking her for her honesty and assistance. I then suggested to Dave to go downstairs and find the caretaker and show the photograph of Plum to him. If he positively identified it, then we would need a statement from him.

I needed to now get some legal backing. Aware that Jean and Malcolm were to meet the lawyers at three o'clock that same afternoon in London, I quickly drove to the railway station and caught a train down to Euston. On the journey south, I felt slightly numbed by the revelation which had just swept over me, like some massive pools win. I'd had my suspicions, but in all honesty, and deep down, I had been finding it difficult to accept a man in such a high-ranking position as, Adrian Plum, could swoop so low as to commit murder. The man's ego had obviously provided a sense of invulnerability, and by trying to be clever, he had in fact, finally been caught out by the truthfulness of one small and fragile young lady.

Within a couple of hours or so, I was travelling in a taxi across the capital, heading for where I knew I would find, Jean and Malcolm, and the defence lawyers. My mind was now focused on a multitude of ifs and buts. What if the caretaker failed to identify Plum from his photograph? Would that one young girl's statement be sufficient to convict, against the robust and powerful resilience of a Deputy Chief Constable? Other scenarios would need to be addressed, but I found myself smiling, as I peered out of the taxi window. My main source of relief was that we were on the brink of a major success story.

I found my two associates sitting with, John Mitchell in a narrow corridor, outside the office of Mr. Bertram Lake QC, the man who had accepted the commission to defend, Jean at her trial. Obviously, all three were surprised to see me, but before I could say a word, the office door opened and the learned counsel with the wavy grey hair appeared, smiling pleasantly.

"I am so sorry to have kept you waiting," he apologised, "Please do come in."

The solicitor led the way and I followed with, Jean and Malcolm sandwiched between us. She surreptitiously turned and whispered to me, "We've been waiting here for nigh on two bloody hours," knowing that with my low level of patience, I would have been off long before then, and her barrister would have had to earn his money by visiting me in my own back yard.

We all sat at the usual long, oval conference table with the QC facing me.

"I'm afraid we haven't met," he said in a stern voice, as though assuming I had stepped into the wrong room but failing to offer his hand. Perhaps he suspected I was contaminated with some dreadful tropical disease.

John Mitchell immediately introduced me.

"And what role does he have to play in all of this?" the senior lawyer enquired, quite aggressively, or so I thought. In fact, considering I had some vital information to share with them, I felt pretty pissed off by the man's conceited manner. For all he knew, I could very well have been waiting with the others outside his office, for the past couple of nauseating hours. No, he didn't impress me at all.

John Mitchell appeared to be slightly embarrassed and dumbfounded by the question and hesitated with an answer.

"Well," the man said, raising his voice, "Is he in, or is he out?"

That was enough for me. I answered for the others by standing from my seat, and quickly explaining to Jean, and Jean alone, that we had achieved some tremendous success and could now prove that she had been the victim of a conspiracy. I enjoyed doing that, if only to put the

London lawyer in his place and twisted the knife further by confirming to the lady, I would wait for her outside. Then I made for the door, but didn't actually exit, until I had turned around and spoke a few more words of encouragement.

"But don't waste too much time with this chappie," I said with some sarcasm, "Because I don't think you will be needing him." At that I left four individuals, each of whom sat there with their mouths wide open and their eyes flushed with disbelief.

As soon as I made the corridor outside and was pacing my way down towards the main reception, I heard both, Jean and, John Mitchell racing after me.

"What is it? What success have you had?" she frantically asked.

I then took it upon myself to enjoy the moment, and teased her by looking at Jean, and then at her solicitor, before suggesting, "Shall we go for a coffee, and I shall reveal all, my dear?"

Her solicitor became flustered. "What about..." He looked over his shoulder at the open door leading to Bertram Lake's office, and then agreed, "Why not."

Malcolm Richards had overheard it all and was quickly on his feet following us down the corridor, leaving the Learned Counsel without a client.

"I hate cheeky kids," I quipped, as we walked away from the Inns of Court.

The small coffee house just around the corner from the Royal Courts of Justice, was a lot more welcoming than the atmosphere inside that arrogant man's office, and all three of them sat listening intently, as I described everything that had taken place, leaving out my visit to see the Chief Constable of a neighbouring force. Finally, when I had finished, Jean leant over and gave me a bit kiss on one cheek, and Malcolm shook my hand, but I noticed how cautious and wary, John Mitchell remained. I asked him the reason, why?

"The allegations are of the most serious nature," he answered, "And we only have one witness, a young girl at that, you say, who has identified a current Deputy Chief Constable as being a potential suspect for a murder."

I held up a hand and stopped the solicitor from continuing, before phoning Dave Stewart.

"Any luck with the caretaker, Dave?" I asked.

"Christ, he's offered to draw a better picture of him for us. He's positively identified Plum as having seen him visit the tower block on a number of occasions, including on the same day as the murder took place. I can't shut him up."

"Have you got a statement from him?"

"I'm in the middle of doing that at the moment. I've just nipped out to take this call."

After speaking with the lad, I turned to all three and reiterated what, Dave had told me.

"Now we have two independent witnesses identifying our man."

John Mitchell appeared more relaxed and suggested, "Well, for a man in his position, he certainly has a number of questions to answer. How do you intend going about it?"

It was then I told them about my visit to see, Philip Gardiner, and that he had been quite prepared to instigate what proceedings were necessary in the circumstances.

"But why go to all that trouble of trying to destroy me?" Jean asked, "When he could have still got rid of that list without setting me up."

"You were his Nemesis, Jean," I answered, "He feared you more than anybody and somehow had it planted in his mind that, whilst you were still around, he was in danger of losing everything."

"Well, he's in bloody danger of losing it all now," Malcom Richards said.

John Mitchell elected to remain with us, rather than travel back to Bristol, and it was four happy and contented individuals sitting in that train carriage bound for home. The die had been cast and we still had work to do.

Chapter Twenty One

Each and every member of my team was elated by the news we shared with them on the day following our return from London. They had all worked extremely hard for our cause, and I was as pleased for them, as for anyone else, except of course, Jean Goodman herself. There still remained a few loose ends to tie up, mostly relating to locations and opportunity for the suspect to commit his crimes, but those could be dealt with at a later date. As soon as we had spoken with all of our people, and at, John Mitchell's request, some of us were heading back to London.

You see, the problem with chasing felons around the streets and making arrests before charging people with the crimes they have committed, was the fact there was a downside to such exploits, which can be described with one word – paperwork. Although none of us were still live cops, as it were, there was still a need to document all we had put together, in particular statements taken, which incriminated our main suspect. So, we needed to compile a full file containing all the relevant material we had gathered. There was a section containing sufficient evidence to prove beyond doubt, Jean Goodman had been a victim rather than a perpetrator of crime. And another implicating, Adrian Plum, as the man behind the murder of a young prostitute and leading figure in a conspiracy to cover his appalling crime, by implicating the Head of CID in the way he had. With a great deal of help from Jean's solicitor, John Mitchell, after just two days working in a room at a London Hotel, the file was completed. Finally, it appeared that the light at the end of the tunnel was within our grasp.

An appointment was made to once again, meet Philip Gardiner at his Police Headquarters, and together with Miss Goodman's solicitor, we arrived there at the appointed time, where I found my old friend appearing to be more formal than the last time we had met. The Chief Constable had spent most of his career being suspicious of lawyers, and I guessed it was a habit he found hard to break, when confronting, John Mitchell.

After the introductions, we both quickly went through the evidence file with, Phil, who had arranged for one of his Administration Superintendents to also be present. I was certainly impressed by the efficient and knowledgeable way in which the solicitor answered a variety of questions put to him by both senior officers, as we ploughed through the file.

Finally, Phil sat back in his chair, with a wry smile on his face.

"I must say," he glibly remarked, looking straight at me, "You do not appear to have lost any of your tenacity when it comes to investigating such sensitive events as these. I am also impressed by your commitment on behalf of your client, Mr. Mitchell." There, the lawyer from Bristol had managed to turn over what had been a lifetime's derisory attitude towards all members of the Law Society.

"Now you have seen what evidence we have, what advise would you give us?" I asked, hoping for the answer I actually received.

"Mr. Plum's Chief Constable needs to be updated with this information as soon as possible, and if he submits a formal request to the Home Office for my force to undertake the necessary Inquiry, obviously I shall agree."

"There's no way we can move things along quicker then?" I asked, aware that we needed action to be taken before, Jean Goodman's trial date.

"No, but this will only take a matter of hours rather than days. If you leave a copy of this file with us, I will personally contact Christopher Hartley, this afternoon and recommend the appropriate action. Trust me, I shall be asked to commence an independent Inquiry into Mr. Plum's activities."

I was delighted, and yet in a strange way, still angered by what had taken place. I mentioned the inference of some involvement by the Assistant Chief Constable, Anthony Freer, who had visited the flat in which, Julie Roberts was living, and Phil Gardiner assured me that he would leave no stone unturned. That in itself from a man whose word was his bond, was sufficient for me to leave with, John Mitchell, and await the outcome.

For the following couple of days, we all remained on tender hooks, meeting frequently at, Jean Goodman's home. I tried to explain what both her solicitor and, Phil Gardiner had told me in relation to, Adrian Plum having been the despicable man behind the hiring of a professional contract killer. In both their opinions, they believed that, unless he confessed to such a criminal act, there was insufficient evidence to have convicted him. In a way, it didn't matter, as long as the man faced his peers on charges of murder and conspiracy.

Phil Gardiner's team moved extremely quickly, and when I answered the phone to him, I was expecting the Chief Constable to tell me that agreement had been reached for him to conduct the Inquiry into the allegations made against, Adrian Plumb. I was surprised to hear him confirm that, all the necessary enquiries had been completed. Anthony Freer had confessed to visiting the prostitute's flat with his DCC on a number of occasions, for the purposes of sexual activity, and although he denied any involvement in the murder itself, he did provide evidence of, Adrian Plum's scheming and conspiring to cover up the killing, and what he believed was a need to remove, Jean Goodman, from any involvement in the subsequent investigation.

Both Plum and Freer had been suspended from duty and a full evidence file had been submitted by Phil's people to the Crown Prosecutions Service. They would both undoubtedly stand trial, Freer for conspiracy to cover up a crime, and Plum for both conspiracy and murder.

The icing on the cake came when, John Mitchell rang, Jean to inform her that all proceedings against her had been dropped and she was free to return to her old position within her force. I was with her when she received that news, as was Malcolm Richards. Strangely, she appeared subdued, which I could understand, following the roller coaster ride she had just been on.

Just as strangely, but somehow not surprising, the Grainger family disappeared into thin air. Rumour had it, they had left the area altogether, supposedly to search for other victims who could supply them with whatever eerie attention they were seeking.

As a mark of gratitude to all concerned, Jean paid for a celebratory meal at her favourite nearby Chinese Restaurant, inviting every member of my team, and of course, Malcolm Richards who had never really left her side throughout her ordeal.

I ploughed my way through my Chow Mein, watching the laughter coming from her, as she shared jokes with the remainder of the company, and witnessed all the stress and traumatic pressure quickly dissolving to take advantage of that social event. What she had earlier confided in me was that her Chief Constable had offered to pay her a substantial amount of money, in recompense for the anxiety and victimisation from which she had so cruelly suffered.

Towards the end of the evening, Jean raised a glass of champagne and drank to my health, at the same time, thanking everyone present for helping her through her nightmare. Whether the lady would require continuation of her psychiatric treatment, was something for Jean to consider later, but there was no doubting the most effective therapy she had received was the result and outcome of the investigation others had conducted on her behalf.

For my part, I raised a glass to each and every one of my team, without whose valuable assistance, we would never have achieved true justice.

I drove, Jean home after the event, only to find the lady strangely subdued. At one stage of the journey, I actually thought she had fallen asleep. But then, quite unexpectedly she admitted, "I have thirty years police service in now. Do I really want to go back to them, after all that's happened?" It was a statement of intent, rather than a question, and I just nodded.

"After what has happened, I find I no longer have the same motivation or enthusiasm to continue working for that organisation." She looked directly across at me, and confessed, "I intend submitting my retirement papers in the morning."

I fully understood how she was feeling and couldn't blame her.

"Any idea what you will do, after all, the police family has been your life?"

She paused, before quietly answering.

"I was wondering if there were any vacancies at your newspaper for another feature writer."

My surprise was evident, but after a moment, we both began to laugh at the idea.

The police service was about to lose a valuable and extremely professional lady, and for what purpose? All in the name of self-preservation by one man who believed he was superior to everyone else and was convinced he could get away with murder. That, I thought, would be a good ending to the story I would begin writing up later that night, in readiness for submission to a very patient editor. One thing was certain, I would ensure a full-blown portrait of, Adrian Plum would cover the front page. It was also possible, I might even consider picking up the threads of my research into Hostage Negotiators, but there again, somehow my interest in that particular story had somewhat dwindled.

About the Author

John F Plimmer retired from the West Midlands force as a prominent high-profile detective following a thirty-one-year illustrious career in which he was responsible for the investigation of more than 30 murder inquiries, all of which were detected successfully.

Following his retirement, he lectured in Law at Birmingham University and became a columnist and feature writer for The Sunday Mercury and Birmingham Evening Mail. Today he frequently participates in discussions and interviews on police and legal subjects on both television and radio. His television work has involved working as a script consultant on a number of popular crime dramas.

His published works include a number of Home Office Blue Papers on Serious Crime Management and Covert Police Handling. He is also the author of a number of published books which include 'In the Footsteps of the Whitechapel Murders' (The Book Guild); Inside Track; Running with the Devil; The Whitechapel Murders and Brickbats & Tutus (House of Stratus).

He is a dedicated reader of Louis L'Amour often giving L'Amour's work as the reason for spending years researching the old pioneering west.

His western novels include 'The Invisible Gun' 'Apache Justice' and 'The Butte Conspiracy'. His book, 'The Cutting Edge' is a partially factual account of the biggest bank hoist ever committed in the history of the United Kingdom. The same work is the first of a seven-book series featuring Dan Mitchell, a British agent working for the Deep Cover Agency of the Foreign Office.

Other published books written by John Plimmer include:

Dan Mitchell series:
Cutting Edge
Red Mist
The Food Mountain
The Neutron Claw
Chinese Extraction
Wrangel Island
Justice Casee

The Victorian Detective's series:
The Victorian Case Review Detective
The Graveyard Murders
A Farthing for a Life

Other books:
Inside Track
Running with the Devil
In the Footsteps of Capone
The World's most Notorious Serial Killers
In the Footsteps of the Whitechapel Murders
Fallen Paragons – The story of the West Midlands Serious Crime Squad
Brickbats & Tutus
Backstreet Urchins
George's War
Hilda's War
A Village at War
Blue Conspiracy

Western Trilogy:
Tatanka Jake
Apache Justice
The Butte Conspiracy

Highwayman series:
In the Footsteps of the Highwaymen
The Wood Cutter
The Return
Four Flushers

37197414R00139

Printed in Poland
by Amazon Fulfillment
Poland Sp. z o.o., Wrocław